AIRSHIP 27 PRODUCTIONS

OCCULT Detectives Volume 1
"Personal Devil" © 2014 Joel Jenkins
"The Strix Society" © 2014 Josh Reynolds
"The Lost Wife of Thomas Tan" © 2014 Jim Beard
"Jazzy" © 2014 Ron Fortier

Published by Airship 27 Productions
www.airship27.com
www.airship27hangar.com

Interior illustrations © 2014 Rob Davis
Cover illustration © 2014 Rob Davis & Jesús Rodríguez

Managing Editor: Ron Fortier
Associate Editor: Charles Saunders
Marketing and Promotions Manager: Michael Vance
Production and design by Rob Davis

ISBN-13: 978-0692344989 (Airship 27)
ISBN-10: 0692344985

Printed in the United States of America

10 9 8 7 6 5 4 3 2 1

OCCULT DETECTIVES VOLUME ONE

PERSONAL DEVIL

A LONE CROW ADVENTURE
BY JOEL JENKINS

Crossing the American River, a few miles below Sutter's Mill where California gold was first discovered, and traveling down the Canyon of the Middle Fork the Indian dressed in cowboy's clothing passed an alder upon which the words *Murderer's Bar* were carved. It was near here on a pebbled sand bar that the remains of a camp had been found by the Merritt-Buckner expedition. The former campsite contained the scorched bones and remnants of both white man and Indian, which had been burned in a pit upon that bar, the hair of both Indian and white man strewn about as if in some sort of ritual.

Even this grisly discovery was not enough to tarnish the lure of gold. Just out of shouting distance of Murderer's Bar a few buildings had sprung up to supply and outfit prospectors who worked the Middle Fork of the American River, panning for flecks and pebbles of gold. It was here that Lone Crow found the tavern owned by the infamous Mormon gunfighter Porter Rockwell. Lone Crow slid from his horse and hitched it at the rail. Inside the incongruent conglomeration of hewed trees and salvaged board from the ramshackle cabin of a deserted mining operation, Crow found Rockwell, nursing an ale. He was sitting on a stool, fashioned from a whiskey crate, at the rough-hewn bar formed by splitting a large tree down the center.

Receding at the top, Porter's dark brown hair spilled over his shoulders. He turned his cold blue gaze upon the man entering his tavern and his somberness was momentarily replaced with a large grin. "Brother Crow, you are a sight for sore eyes!"

The bar was mostly empty at mid-day except for a few miners at the back who had decided to give up their panning in favor of raising three sheets to the wind. Crow pulled up one of the makeshift stools alongside Rockwell, ignoring the suspicious gazes of the miners who wondered why a long-haired Indian had just walked into their bar.

"An urgent message from Porter Rockwell can't be ignored," said Crow.

Rockwell blanched. "Careful when you say my name, Crow. I'm going by Brown, now. There's more than a few Missourians around who would have my head if they knew who I really was."

Crow nodded, understanding this well. "So what is it that brings me here?"

Rockwell appeared a bit sheepish. "I may have overreacted, Crow…and I feel bad about dragging you all the way out here on a fool's errand."

"A fool's errand?" repeated Crow.

"The fool being me. I'm all balled up about the matter."

"What matter?" asked Crow.

"It's just that I'm befuddled by the whole thing, and I don't even understand what happened to me but I know that you've dealt with some weird things, and I've sure 'nuff seen some strange things when I've been in your company. I thought that maybe you'd have some ideas…" Rockwell broke off. "I'm forgetting my manners."

Rockwell called out to the bartender. "Elvin, get Mr. Crow, here, something to drink."

"Water will be fine," said Crow.

Elvin, the squat bartender with the bushy beard seemed confused by this. "But we don't…"

"You heard what he said," barked Rockwell. "Go get the man some water!"

"Yes, sir." Elvin hurried out the back door of the tavern in search of some water — not a common request from their patrons.

Rockwell lifted his half full glass. "You're a better man than I, Crow. I can't seem to stay away from the hard stuff."

Crow knew that despite the Mormon edict against strong drink, Rockwell hadn't completely complied. "So what are these strange things that you've been seeing, Porter?"

"Well, Brigham asked me to collect tithes from Sam Brannan, whose been collecting the moneys from the saints here in California. I went with Brother Lyman to ask for the tithes and he told me that I'd have to present a receipt from God before he handed over those tithes.

"I don't much like being told to skedaddle, so I pulled my hog leg on him. Brannan, he just laughed in my face, and I was about to lay a stripe across his skull with the barrel of my pistol when I looked up and saw some dark thing hovering in the corner over Brannan's head."

"A dark thing?" asked Crow, for he'd seen many dark things in his brief time on the earth.

"I...I think it was a woman, but her body was all swirling blackness, like somebody was stirring a barrel of tar. All I really remember about her is eyes like pits into hell." Porter peered at the Indian. "Have you ever run into something like that before?"

Crow thought long before answering. "Perhaps, maybe a kurdaitcha or a succubus, if the personage was indeed female."

"Best as I could tell," said Rockwell, "but like I said, the body was not solid, it was like gun smoke or some such thing. I've heard of a succubus, but this creature was not desirable in any way that I could tell. Maybe she was a kurdaitcha."

"What happened when you saw the creature?" asked Crow.

"My mind went blank. I couldn't think. I couldn't even act. Finally, Lyman had to lead me away! I've never felt so befuddled; except for maybe when I'm deep in my drinks."

"It could be a kurdaitcha," said Crow. "They are malevolent spirits that have the power to confuse men's minds. Usually, they attach themselves to a host and persuade them to do wicked things and help them accomplish those things."

"You think that this kurdaitcha has attached herself to Sam Brannan?"

Crow gave the slightest of shrugs. "It's possible ... if it is indeed a kurdaitcha."

"So how do you fight a kurdaitcha, Crow? Because I'll be durned if I'm going to go back to Brigham and tell him I couldn't fetch the tithing funds he sent me for."

"You can kill the host." Crow accepted a glass of cold river water from Elvin. "But the kurdaitcha will transfer to the unprotected body of anyone within the distance that a scream can be heard."

"That can be a long ways," said Rockwell. "Is there any way to stop it?"

"By wearing shoes made of emu feathers and human blood," replied Crow, "but emu feathers may be hard to come by in California."

"Human blood is plentiful enough. Is there any other way to stop the kurdaitcha from moving into another body?"

8

JOEL JENKINSJOEL JENKINS

"Maybe or maybe not," said Crow. "I don't even know for sure if emu feather shoes will do the trick."

"You don't know? What did you do last time you encountered one of ..."

Rockwell broke off from his conversation when the beer glass in his hand exploded into shards. Ale foam sprayed the rough-hewn bar top, and the report of a rifle rang in their ears. The bartender clutched at his chest where a blossom of crimson appeared. The first gunshot was followed by more, coming through the open doorway, splintering the bar in a half dozen places while Crow and Rockwell dove for cover deeper in the tavern.

The gold hunters who had been sharing drinks in the corner left the crates upon which they had been perched and crouched behind the tables, which were also constructed from crates and slabs cut from tree stumps.

Rockwell grabbed up a fire poker and began to clear out the mud which was daubed between the seams of the logs which constructed the tavern. "I'll hold them off, Crow, make myself a distraction, while you go out the back and see if you can get a bead on them."

Crow had been of a same mind and was already headed toward the back door of the tavern, which was little more than a doe skin flap. He rolled through in the case that whoever had shot Elvin had an accomplice that was set up and waiting for someone to emerge from the rear of the tavern. This bit of precaution saved Crow's life; for the moment he tumbled into the open, a rifle began to spit at him from the grove of trees that flanked the rudely built assemblage of huts and shanties.

A pair of holes appeared in the doe skin flap and then whoever was firing from the woods adjusted his aim and gouts of dirt and rock erupted near Crow as he scrambled to find cover behind a large bloodstained stump, from which protruded a hatchet amid a pile of chicken heads. Crow could hear gunfire from the front of the cabin, and based on the frequency and sound of the shots he could tell that there were at least two gunmen firing upon the cabin from the front. Rockwell was apparently alive and well, because he was lustily yelling denigrations at the attackers as he returned fire through the chinks between the logs.

Crow wasn't of much help to Rockwell at the moment, because he found himself pinned down by the rifleman at the rear and unable to move from the cover of the stump for fear of being hit. As of yet, he hadn't fired a single shot in return. Part of this was because he hadn't figured out precisely where the rifleman was positioned and the other part was because he didn't want to waste any bullets.

He picked up and tossed a chicken head out into the open and it jumped as a bullet struck it, then Crow reached up and wrenched the hatchet loose from the log, before ducking back behind cover. The stump shuddered as a bullet struck it. Without ever leaving cover, Crow lofted the hatchet in the general direction of the rifleman and then ducked around to the left of the log.

The hatchet was still spinning through the air, and Crow could see the rifleman, crouched behind a fallen tree some twenty yards distant. For a moment, the rifleman's attention was diverted by the flight of the hatchet and amidst a split-second determination of whether it was a danger to him. It was not, however, the blade of the axe that posed the threat to his life. Crow fired his eagle-butted Colt. 45 three times. One of the shots shaved off a scrap of bark from the log over which the rifleman had laid his gun, and the other two shots stitched across the breast and collarbone of the rifleman.

As the hatchet whirled off to be lost in the trees, the rifleman groaned and sank to the ground, his rifle toppling after him. Crow's own rifle was still scabbarded on his horse, and so he raced into the grove, leaping the log behind which the dying rifleman lay. The rifleman looked at him resentfully, as Crow plucked up his rifle. The lips of the dying man fluttered, but he was unable to say anything, before the last of his life's blood spilled to the thirsty earth.

The rifleman had just finished loading a fresh cartridge and Crow jerked loose the dead man's bandolier of ammunition and threw it over his own shoulder. Without hesitating he ran along the back of a supply outpost and a dilapidated shack held together with clots of mud and rope salvaged from an abandoned ship in the port of San Francisco, and peered around the edge, rifle thrown to his shoulder.

Black powder vapor undulated through the chinks of the tavern as Rockwell fired up the craggy rise and into the forest. However, it was the puffs of black powder that rose from the forest that interested Crow, for these indicated the positions of the pair of riflemen that hid in the copse of slender trees that grew thick along the slopes.

In order to steady his aim, Crow rested the barrel of the rifle on a stick that protruded from the corner of the shack. The shot was a tricky one because he had to thread the bullet through the screen of tree trunks to hit a sniper whose head and shoulders were the only parts of his body that were visible, and which were partially concealed by the boles of intervening saplings.

Crow blew out a breath so that the rise and fall of his lungs would not throw off his aim and he squeezed the trigger. The bullet took off the hat of the rifleman, who clapped a hand to his scalp. When his palm came away bloody, he began to scramble toward the crest of the slope, rifle in his right hand. It took Crow but a moment to pull back the bolt, eject the spent casing and push another into its place. By this time the rifleman was scrambling over the lip of the hill and the second gunman had turned his rifle away from the tavern and toward Crow.

Just over Crow's head, a bullet took a clod of earth and sod off the roof of the shack. Instead of shooting the retreating rifleman, Crow turned his attention to the better concealed rifleman who had remained on the slope. Again, the shot was nigh on impossible. However, Crow managed to skin the bark of a sapling just left of the rifleman, and this sent him ducking out of sight while he reloaded.

While Crow raced to reload before the concealed rifleman could, Rockwell was not disposed to pass up a shot at the momentarily exposed gunman at the top of the ridge. There was still a mass of branches and leaves obscuring the target, but Rockwell's pistol cracked twice and the second round took the rifleman in the heel, splitting his boot, before he staggered over the rise and out of sight.

Crow was quicker on the reload than his opponent who was still hunkered down on the slope, and when that rifleman rose, the Indian adjusted his aim a fraction to the right and sent a bullet skimming down the length of his enemy's rifle barrel and through his right eye. As the rifleman died, he pulled the trigger and blew off another clot of sod, raining dirt down upon the brim of Crow's hat.

Seeing the way was clear, Rockwell emerged from the tavern, even as he replaced some spent cartridges in his pistol. He and Crow each sprinted across the rutted street and threw themselves into the midst of the forested slope, using their momentum to propel them up the uneven and treacherous incline. When they emerged from the forest at the crest of the slope, they caught sight of a pinto, with a white sock on his left rear leg, and its rider which were just about to disappear around the narrow neck of a fissure in the rocky crags.

Rockwell sent a parting bullet in the direction of the fleeing horseman, but it spanged off an outcropping of rock just as the rifleman rounded the corner into the obscurity of the rugged landscape. As the cloud of black gunpowder from his pistol rose, Rockwell glanced back at the remaining horse, which strained at its tether, attempting to uproot the sapling to which it was tied. "It seems you're richer one horse, Crow."

"Sell it and give the proceeds to the bartender's family," said Crow.

"They'll have more need of it than I."

Rockwell nodded. "Elvin was a good man. I don't relish the thought of breaking the bad news to his wife."

"So, just who is it that wants you dead, Porter?"

Rockwell shrugged. "I've kilt a lot of people, never anyone that didn't need killing, but it wouldn't be surprising that someone wanted me dead. There's too many Missourian gold hunters who might remember that I kilt more than a few of their mobocrat friends."

Crow picked his way down the slope. "Maybe your identity isn't as secret as you thought."

"Maybe," conceded Rockwell. "Maybe it's time I take my grubstake and head for friendlier parts."

Crow crouched over the dead rifleman and the gory mess that stained the earth of the slope. He saw the glint of a chain beneath the flannel collar of the man's shirt and he opened up the neck to pull loose a brass medallion that was pressed with the image of the sword-bearing woman with a scale in her left hand, and on the other a large eye around which radiated beams of light or energy. "Does this look familiar to you, Porter?"

"Hmph," grunted Rockwell as he took and examined the coin. "This woman looks like lady justice … except she's missing the blindfold."

"So, justice that is not blind," said Crow as he considered the wide-open eye on the reverse side of the medallion.

"Could have something to do with the Committee of Vigilance." Rockwell viewed the dead body. "Though why they'd be coming after me, I can't say."

Crow was aware of the Committee of Vigilance. "Don't they operate mostly inside of San Francisco?"

Rockwell scratched at his magnificently bearded chin. "That's what I thought, and mostly against those Sydney Ducks which keep setting fire to the city. Most of the judges and politicians are too crooked to do anything about them; leastwise when they are getting paid to look the other way."

"I understood that the Committee was in the habit of dragging the accused before a jury and holding court before deciding what to do with the accused. They just started taking shots at you … without giving you a chance to surrender yourself."

"Maybe this fellow was acting on his own initiative."

"One way to find out," said Crow. "I killed a second man behind your tavern."

Rockwell's sharp blue eyes focused on Crow. "I catch your drift."

In short order they stood over the dead man behind the tavern and Rockwell pulled open his shirt to reveal a similar brass medallion hanging about his neck. "It seems the Committee of Vigilance has something against me. I figure that gives me two options."

"And which option makes the most sense?" asked Crow.

"To turn tail and run," said Rockwell. "But then again, I've never had much common sense. I think I'll ride into San Francisco and find out just what the Committee of Vigilance has against me and see if I can't straighten it out."

"And if they won't listen?"

Rockwell patted his revolver, which he had holstered at his belt. "I can be very persuasive, Crow. Very persuasive."

"I'll ride with you," said Crow. "It seems to me that an extra gun might provide an additional amount of persuasion and the ride will give me some time to consider best how to handle Samuel Brannan and the kurdaitcha that has taken over his body."

"Eh, so now you're sure that it's a kurdaitcha?" questioned Rockwell.

"I'm only sure of one thing: that when it comes to beings of the outer darkness one can never be sure."

Crow and Rockwell paused their horses amidst the clustered tents of the Chicano harlots and migrant gold hunters atop Telegraph Hill and looked down at the San Francisco sprawl—rom the dangerous streets of Sydney Town to Nob Hill, where recently rebuilt structures of brick and wood were going up. The harbor was strewn with ships abandoned by their crews in the delirium of gold fever, and a number of these had been scuttled and salvaged for wood which was used to build some of the lean-tos and shanties that dotted the city.

Crow's face was hard and grim as a cool wind whipped off the waters and gusted up the hill, billowing the canvas of the tents and pushing back his dark hair.

"Something wrong?" asked Rockwell, noting the Indian's expression.

"I've lost the rifleman's trail," replied the Indian.

Rockwell leaned on the horn of his saddle. "So have I. Too much traffic through these here parts, and the ground here's too hard, but I reckon if we continued down the hill a bit we'll pick up his trail."

Crow gently nudged his horse forward and it proceeded down the winding trail. He stopped suddenly, when he saw a pinto tethered to a pole just beyond a cluster of four tents, which formed just a few stars of the constellation of tents which covered the hillside.

Rockwell, likewise, did not fail to see the pinto. "That horse looks mighty familiar, Crow."

"You think it might have a sock on its left rear leg?"

"There's only one way to find out." Rockwell slipped off his horse and tethered it to a pole driven into the earth alongside the path.

Crow, likewise, tethered this horse to the same pole. Then each took a different path toward the pinto, Rockwell threading through a series of tents at the upward slope of the hill, while Crow approached on the path that the horse had used, for now he could again clearly see the prints of its shoes. Just by seeing the prints of the horseshoes Crow could see that this was the horse they had followed from Murderer's Bar, because the front right shoe had a nick which was visible in the print. So confirming that the left rear leg of the pinto wore a white sock was merely a formality. This was the horse of one of the men who had killed Elvin.

As they threaded through the other tents, avoiding the staked lines, a few of the occupants, having heard the sound of the tethered horses, emerged from their tents. "I'm open for business, boys!" called a buxom woman with dusky skin and a cascade of black hair.

Her sister in trade, with rouged cheeks and dark eyes, called from the flap of another tent. "Over here. I can make you a bargain!"

Crow glanced back and when she saw his face she clapped a hand over her mouth and staggered back into her tent. At first, Crow thought it might be because of his garb she had expected a white man or a Mexican, but instead she had seen the face of an Indian. But then the other harlot began to cry out.

"It is the *el mago pistolero!*" She, too, retreated into the imaginary safety of her tent.

Rockwell halted in front of the tent next to the tethered pinto. "The magic *pistolero*? It seems you've gained quite a reputation for yourself."

"No worse a reputation than yourself," said Crow, for he had heard the name of Porter Rockwell uttered, and often accompanied by a curse word, far and wide. "Part of the problem is I was involved in a gunfight with some immortals on this very hill."

"Resurrected beings?" asked Rockwell.

"Not in the sense of the great and final resurrection," said Crow. "These were evil folks imbued with unnatural vitality and life."

"And where are they now?"

"Mostly dead," said Crow, and as Rockwell moved around the perimeter of the tent he ducked to the side and shook the flap of the tent. Immediately, a volley of gunfire punched three holes through the tent flap. It was as Crow had feared: the hawking cries of the Chileno harlots had alerted their quarry and ruined any chance they had at taking him unawares.

Crow didn't dare return fire into the tent, without clearly seeing his target, for fear that he might hit an innocent occupant. He fired a couple of bullets into the air, to keep the gunman's attention, even while he moved behind the pinto, who let out a bray of fear. Apparently, the gunman inside the tent didn't share the same fear about hitting innocents outside and he fired in the direction of Crow's gunshots, putting three bullets into the flank of his horse, who let out a scream, jerked loose the pole to which he was tethered and lurched through the forest of tents, knocking down six of them before giving a heaving convulsion and falling down dead.

Rockwell used this diversion and slit an opening in the opposite wall of the tent with his Bowie knife, and slipped inside. The gunman, who had a bandaged poultice on his scalp where a bullet had creased him, was facing away from Rockwell and emptying the spent shell casings from his pistol. A Chileno woman with wavy hair and a low-cut dress fashioned from burlap sat on the floor, face to her knees and arms wrapped around her head, so she didn't see as Rockwell slipped up behind the gunman and put a knife to his throat.

"Drop the pistol or I'll bleed your jugular."

The gunman let his pistol fall to the dirt floor and the woman peered through the tangle of her arms and fingers. She slowly began to scuttle backward toward the slit in the tent.

She gave out a gasp and changed her direction when she saw Crow step through the same cut through which she was hoping to escape.

Rockwell offered her a side-eyed glance. "You stay put, Darling. Keep nice and quiet and be cooperative-like and you won't get hurt."

She nodded and Rockwell spun the gunman onto a crate, the slats buckling beneath his posterior as his weight came down on it. He saw a pistol in Rockwell's other hand and peered down the recesses of the dark barrel that was pointed between his eyes.

"I would like to know," said Rockwell, "why I can't even sit down in my own tavern and enjoy a drink without having some penny-ante gunman try to shoot me down."

"I...I didn't mean nothing by it," said the gunman. "It...It warn't personal."

"I beg to differ," said Rockwell. "I take it very personal when my bartender takes a bullet, meant for me, in the chest, because the person firing the rifle doesn't have the guts to get close enough to do the job right."

The gunman opened his mouth to defend himself, but he couldn't seem to find any words that would do the trick.

"Why did you come gunning for me?" asked Rockwell.

"You're famous," stuttered the gunman. "I'd make a name for myself if I managed to shoot you down!"

"Yes, you would," admitted Rockwell, "and then some wet-behind-the-ears puke would come gunning for you and try to shoot *you* in the back."

Crow hadn't said anything to this point, but now he flipped the brass medallion he had retrieved from one of the dead men, so that it dropped between the gunman's feet. "If you have any desire to live, tell us the truth. What does this symbol mean?"

"It's a symbol that means a person belongs to the San Francisco Committee of Vigilance," said the gunman from his perch upon the broken crate. "We hunt down criminals and bring them to justice. I was told you was the worst of the worst, Porter Rockwell."

"And yet I've had the forbearance to keep from killing you, as yet," replied Rockwell. "Just who was it that told you I was a criminal that was so bad you needed to kill me outright instead of dragging me to trial?"

"Why, it was Sam Brannan," said the gunman. "He said that you was wanted for the killing of Governor Boggs of Missouri!"

Rockwell's face tightened and his voice was exasperated. "I didn't kill Governor Boggs. He's still alive to this day which should prove to anyone with half a brain that I wasn't the one who took the shot at him!"

The gunman's face took on a perplexed expression. "Governor Boggs is still alive?"

"Yes, may his soul rot in hell."

Crow glanced out the slit in the tent. " I wasn't aware that Samuel Brannan was behind the Vigilance Committee."

Now, it didn't take much coaxing to draw words out of the gunman. His lips moved freely. "He is one of the founders and asked me to join a secret society within the committee that would go against criminals that not even the rest of the Vigilance Committee would dare touch!"

Crow's face was impassive. "So, Brannan told you that Porter Rockwell was such a bad man that he needed to be killed outright ..."

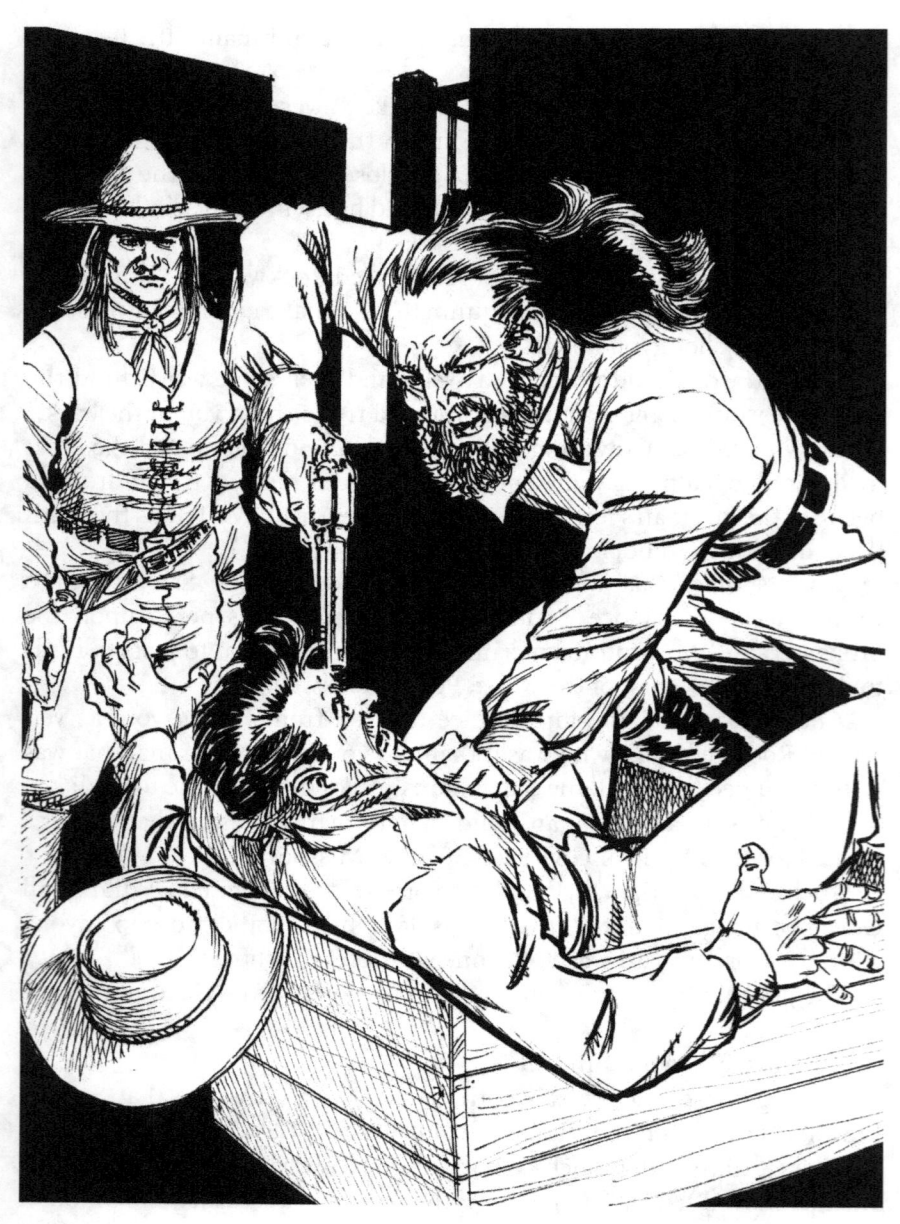

"I...I didn't mean nothing by it. It...It warn't personal."

"That's what he said," agreed the gunman, "and he impressed upon us how dangerous a man Rockwell was to face."

"What other secret killings have you done for Brannan?" asked Rockwell.

"Men who was threatening to kill him," said the gunman. "A man doesn't get to be rich, powerful and influential like Brannan without jealous people wanting to take what's his."

Rockwell snorted. "Or attracting people that will do anything, including murder, to ride on your coat-tails. Brannan got rich by taking what wasn't rightfully his and treading on any in his way."

"Is Governor Boggs really still alive?" asked the gunman.

"Unfortunately, yes," said Rockwell. "Now get up and give me your hands. I'm going to take you in for the murder of Elvin Woods."

The gunman was perspiring profusely. The Vigilance Committee was at odds with the corrupt San Francisco officials and they would gladly make an example of a member of the Vigilance Committee with a swift trial and a hanging. "I wasn't the one that fired the bullet that killed your bartender! It was Mortimer that fired that shot!"

Rockwell jerked the gunman to his feet and began binding his hands, while Crow kept a gun trained upon him. "I'll let you argue your case to a jury. Best of luck with that."

Crow frowned as he felt a darkness descend upon his mind. He glanced outside the tent again, and saw some of the local denizens of Telegraph Hill had gathered on the winding path and were gesturing in the direction of the demolished tents and the dead Pinto that lay amidst the wreckage of one of them. Still, they had not mustered the courage to approach the source of the gunfire.

A cursing Chileno harlot and a half-dressed customer were dragging themselves from the wreckage of her ruined tent, but none of this might have caused the troubling pall that had fallen upon Crow's soul. There was some devilish force at work, but he could not locate the source or cause of the psychic disturbance that he felt. "We need to pony up. There's trouble coming."

"How many men?" asked Rockwell as he cinched the bonds tight around the gunman's wrists.

"Not that kind of trouble," said Crow.

Rockwell's brow furrowed. "Then what kind of trouble are we talking, Crow?"

"Big evil." Even as Crow said the words a dark mist descended and the earth began to tremble. Outside, the gathered inhabitants of Telegraph

Hill cried out in terror and scattered to the imagined safety of their canvas and animal skin tents and ramshackle huts.

"It's just a trembler," said Rockwell. "They have them all the time on the coast. The ground's unsteady here."

Crow could feel icy fingers clawing at his soul. "It's more than a trembler, Porter."

A wicked grin grew on the gunman's face and with the split heel of his boot he stepped on top of the wide-eyed talisman of the Committee of Vigilance which was still on the dirt floor of the tent. "Sam Brannan swore that nothing would be able to harm us. He said that She would protect her templar knights—her sacred defenders!"

"There is nothing sacred about her." Crow widened his stance so that the shaking earth did not pitch him to the ground.

Rockwell reeled backward and fell on his posterior, and the Chileno harlot began to crawl beneath the back wall of the tent, but when she saw the swirling mists of darkness that descended, blotting out the noonday sun, she gave out a horrified cry and dared not leave the tent. Amidst this, only the bound gunman seemed unshaken by the congealing darkness and the heaving earth. He stood straight, unaffected and unfazed by the turmoil.

The walls of the tent began to rattle. The earth groaned and the thickening fog returned a moaning cry that chilled the blood in Crow's veins. The Chileno's limbs shook and she let out a piercing scream as the darkness reached out and tore the tent away, leaving only the quivering framework and poles, and exposing the four occupants to the chill tendrils of creeping mist which began to close in upon them.

A frost began to form on Crow's flesh and he could see ice crawling across the barrel of Rockwell's drawn gun barrel and forming in his beard. The pitch fingers of mist began to entwine with the Chileno woman's raven dark hair, turning the locks into a filigree of icicles. She batted frantically at the clutching fingers, but succeeded only in breaking off frozen strands of her own hair, and they scattered across the frozen ground in sparkling shards.

Only the gunman was unaffected. No grasping fog touched him and no chill touched his flesh or garments. "She takes care of her own! She will crush her enemies! She will rise again!"

The bitter cold began to seep into Crow's limbs, numbing his nerves so that he could scarcely feel his own fingers or toes. The cold was growing in such intensity that Crow knew it would be just moments before he was unable to even lift his own feet. So, with the last movements that he could muster from his crepitated limbs he hurled himself at the unaffected gunman who appeared to be immune to the supernatural forces that were assailing them.

The gunman's laugh was cut short as Crow smashed into him, the layer of frost that had been forming on the Indian's hat and clothing leaping free as he struck. The gunman was knocked off his feet and went rolling outside the perimeter where the tent had once stood. The cold was unbearable and, lying on the ground, Crow saw the wide-eyed talisman of the Committee of Vigilance sitting on the chill ground, untouched by the frost that was forming on every stool, belonging, or item of cast-off clothing that belonged to the Chileno harlot.

Rockwell attempted to run from the freeze, thinking that perhaps if he could make it to the trail, gravity and momentum might carry him down the hill, out of the pervasive influence of the dark fog which had descended upon them, and into the natural heat of the day. He took three strides before his numbed legs took a misstep and he fell hard upon his shoulders, casting a spray of broken ice from his duster.

The scared exhalations of the Chileno plumed into the air, the moisture in her breath turning to frost and falling to the ground. And now that the gunman no longer stood at the center of the tent, his arms grew heavy with hanging icicles and the poultice on his scalp became a cap of ice. Crow reached out toward the untouched talisman, using every bit of will he could dredge from the bottom of his soul to push his fingers forward, so that they crawled toward the shining emblem. Finally the tip of his forefinger touched the emblem and warmth surged through him, chasing away the frigid pall that threatened to overcome him.

With some feeling and strength returning to his limbs, he clutched the talisman in his hands and rolled to his right, coming up alongside of Rockwell and pressing the brass coin against the Mormon's flesh. Immediately the ice that covered Rockwell's duster and hat began to melt away and mighty coughs racked his body.

Crow had come to Rockwell's rescue none too soon, for when he cast his eyes back to the Chileno, he found that she was frozen into place. No flesh could be seen and her body was as if carved from a solid block of ice with the greatest of detail, so that every strand of hair and every pore of her skin had been painstakingly reproduced from life. No breath trickled from between those icy lips, no breath heaved her bosom, and no spark of life remained within her.

Rockwell gave a cry and managed to raise his pistol, even as he caught sight of the gunman, who had killed Elvin, attempting to lift his rifle, which he had somehow managed to retrieve from the spot where the corner of the tent wall had once stood. Shreds of canvas waved in the spectral mist as the ice-laden gunman attempted to fire with frosted trigger finger, but even as he made the attempt his flesh and bone turned to ice from that fearsome chill brought on by the caliginous mists. So when a bullet sped from Rockwell's pistol, the gunman shattered into a thousand frozen fragments of flesh and blood, which cascaded across the hard ground.

Then, as suddenly as the brume miasma had descended upon them, it began to dissipate, dark tendrils seeping away, seeking lower ground or dissolving. The quaking earth ceased its convulsions and the crowd, most of which had been cast to the ground, who had witnessed the malevolent attack climbed to their feet and trekked toward what they hoped would be safer locales. A few remained, awestruck, by the dark manifestation they had just witnessed, sitting dumbfounded and gaping on the ground.

Rockwell regarded the wreckage of the tent and the Chileno woman whose body and visage were still frozen into the icy aspect of fear. "Is there anything we can do for her?"

Crow examined the frozen form of the harlot, face dispassionate. "If we touch her we risk shattering her, like you shattered the gunman. There's nothing we can do."

The Indian relinquished the brass talisman which had saved them from being turned into ice and Rockwell turned it in his calloused fingers. "At least we know of something that can help us combat this demonic thing that attacked us."

Crow was less optimistic. "There's no magic in the thing, and it's no proof against the powers of the kurdaitcha."

"So this dark mist that swallowed us up like hell itself was the kurdaitcha?"

"Sent by the kurdaitcha," corrected Crow. "The kurdaitcha are ancient malevolent spirits that possess the bodies of the weak-minded, sinners, or those who have invited them. They have the power to cloud and affect men's minds, but the more ancient of them sometimes have power over the elements."

Rockwell shook the beading droplets of melted ice from the brim of his hat. "The elements? You mean this kurdaitcha can control earth, water, and fire?"

"The other possibility is air," said Crow, "but I've never heard of a case where the kurdaitcha has sway over more than one element. Yet, it seems that this one has some minor control over the earth as well as water, since she can freeze the moisture in the air or even within our bodies."

"Minor control over the earth?" exclaimed Rockwell. "I wouldn't call the trembler we just experienced *minor control*."

"If she had more than minor control she would have opened the earth up beneath us so that it swallowed us up," said Crow.

Rockwell replaced the hat on his head and examined the unblindfolded face of justice on the amulet. "Say what you want about this brass coin, but it saved us from being frozen into ice statues, so there must be something about it."

"I suspect that the amulet's been marked by the kurdaitcha," said Crow, "so that from afar she will know not to exert her powers against the bearer of it. Once we are in her presence she will know not to exclude the bearer of the coin from her destructive powers … or even once she receives message that she failed to slay us."

Concern crossed Rockwell's bearded face. "So, you're saying that she might at some point be able to use this talisman to locate us and direct her dark, freezing fogs against us?"

Crow nodded. "That's what I'm saying."

Rockwell drew back his arm and chucked the talisman as far as his arm would allow him. It glinted over the sea of tents that sprawled along the hillside, and then disappeared into the brambles and scrub brush of a rocky ravine. "Good riddance to it."

Crow said nothing as he looked out over the bay of listing ships abandoned in the rush for gold, wondering at the madness and fever that gold and greed caused in men.

"Is there anything we can do to beat back the demon that has taken up residence in Sam Brannan?" asked Rockwell. "I'm no coward, but this sort of thing is well beyond my ken. Perhaps we should consult Brother Brigham for the best way to defeat this demon."

"Brigham is in Utah and the kurdaitcha is here, with us," said Crow. "If we delay, we may return to find San Francisco an utter desolation. A kurdaitcha delights in the misery and bloodshed of mankind and she is gathering her power. Once gathered I am sure she will not hesitate to unleash it."

"You mean it gets worse?" questioned Rockwell.

"It was a kurdaitcha that caused the desolation and disappearance of the Roanoke Island colony," said Crow. "The name of that particular kurdaitcha was Naotaorc."

Rockwell was familiar with the story of the British Colony where ninety men, seventeen women, and eleven children had disappeared without a trace. "That was hundreds of years ago. How would you even know that?"

"Such things are recorded in ancient tomes which are kept in the libraries of the Miskatonic University," said Crow. "There are many secrets there which would have been better off destroyed—like the corrupt combinations and pacts of the Gadiantons."

"So how do we fight something that can befuddle our minds and freeze our flesh and bone, Crow?"

"How does one combat the elements?" asked Crow.

"That's exactly what I'm asking," said Rockwell.

Crow returned to his horse and climbed into his saddle.

Scowling, Rockwell followed. "Where are we going, Crow?"

"We're going to find Sam Brannan and exorcise his kurdaitcha."

Rockwell grabbed the saddle horn and swung onto his horse. "Swell, let's ride blindly to our doom. It seems I've got nothing better to do today."

—⫸⫷—

At the corner of Washington and Kearny Streets stood the Bella Union, primarily a gambling hall, but also equipped with a stage for various vaudevillian theatrical, dancing, and vocal performances. Even as Crow and Rockwell approached the entrance, the jangling of a piano filtered into the street, as did the muted tones of both a male and female singer. Because of the high rates of pay available on the California coast, some of the top flight establishments like this were able to attract talent that habitually stayed cloistered in New York or Boston.

Rockwell fingered a small vial which he had obtained from Hell Haggerty, proprietor of the Fierce Grizzly, which was known for the female grizzly bear it kept chained in the street outside, in the Sydney Town portion of San Francisco. "You sure this is going to work, Crow?"

"I don't know," said Crow. "I've never used knockout drops on anybody."

Rockwell raised an eyebrow. "That's not what I'm worried about. Haggerty says these knock a person out in about five minutes and make them easy pickings to rob. Apparently, he uses them all the time in his various establishments."

"You keep some interesting company, Porter."

"You know I don't condone such sort of thing, but he does prove useful" said Rockwell. "Haggerty and I have an understanding since that night I put a bullet through a man who was about to put a knife to his throat. He lets me know when I've got folks gunning for me and is always happy to do me a favor."

"So why didn't he let you know that the Committee of Vigilance was hunting you down?"

Rockwell laughed. "Haggerty and the Committee of Vigilance run in different circles. When their paths cross it usually calls for bullets and arson." They paused a dozen feet away from the entrance of the Bella Union, not drawing near to a group of revelers who were taking bets and enjoying sport at the expense of two drunken fellows brawling in the street. "What I want to know is if these knockout drops will allow us to take down Brannan without releasing the kurdaitcha to take up residence in someone else's body ... or our own, for that matter."

"That's something that I don't know," said Crow, "but perhaps if we can subdue Brannan quietly, we won't arouse the kurdaitcha, and we can take him somewhere isolated to dispose of the demon that possesses him."

"And if the kurdaitcha attempts to enter us?" asked Rockwell.

"We're men of faith, Rockwell. Put your faith in the Lord Jesus Christ that He will protect us."

"And what of Brannan?" asked Rockwell. "Why didn't his faith in Christ protect him?"

"He abandoned that faith, didn't he?" asked Crow. "Can you expect protection from Christ when you've made it clear that you want no part of Him?"

"I suppose not," replied Rockwell.

Rockwell paid a quarter for admission to the Bella Union, but when Crow proffered his quarter the doorman held out an arm, blocking his entrance. "This establishment ain't for redskins. You want to be entertained; you go down to Sydney Town and find some dive that will accept the likes of you."

Turning slightly, hand on the butt of his gun, Rockwell addressed the doorman. "That's Lone Crow you've got your grubby little hand on doorman. He's killed dozens of men far more dangerous than you."

The doorman hesitated, for he'd heard the name of Lone Crow, and how he'd killed Butch Cassidy by slitting his throat with a Bowie knife.

Rockwell continued. "I'd suggest that you accept his quarter and let him inside without any further fuss, and then maybe we can all forget this ugly incident ever happened."

The doorman considered this and removed his hand from Crow's chest. "I do apologize; I didn't recognize you Mr. Crow."

Without speaking, Crow pressed the quarter into the doorman's palm and brushed past him into the smoke-filled interior. Card games progressed at every corner and table of the establishment, and on a stage fringed by red velvet curtains, a dapper man with slicked back hair made a frenzied play at the piano keys while a shapely woman with carefully coiffured golden hair belted out an irreverent tune. Crow had little use for gambling or alcohol, but he found himself fascinated by the piano and the chanteuse so much that Rockwell had to get his attention.

"There's an empty table over there, Crow. Sit tight and I'll see if I can locate Brannan."

The songstress warbled a version of 'Molly Do You Love Me?' and 'I Have Got the Blues Today' and to Crow it seemed scarce but a few figments of time before Rockwell returned to the table bearing a couple bottles of sarsaparilla.

"It took some doing to get these, Crow. It seems this establishment is strictly alcoholic. Normally, I might indulge in one or two tipples myself, but out of respect to you and the job we've got to do this evening I thought…"

"Who's that singer?" asked Crow.

"Sarah Armstridge," said Rockwell. "A pretty piece of calico, if I've ever seen one, but more trouble than a bucket full of weasels in a hen house or so I hear. But then there isn't a woman in this place that wouldn't bleed a man dry and leave him dying in a gulch for fairer prospects. Now listen, one of the house girls by the name of Elsa has told me that Brannan is in a private box on the second floor. He and his friends are being entertained by some others of the house girls, and drinking enough ale to float a ship."

"How do we slip the knockout drops into his drink?" asked Crow.

"Elsa says she's friends with the girls doing the entertaining. For fifteen dollars, Elsa says that she can persuade Charlotte to dose Brannan's drink and let us know when he starts sawing logs."

Crow rolled a small diamond onto the table. "I'm nearly out of cash. Will this be sufficient?"

Rockwell picked it up and examined it in the lantern light. "More than sufficient. Where did you get this?"

"I know of a field of them here in California," said Crow. "There are plenty more if you're interested."

"Interested? Why if I manage to live through this evening I say we saddle up and you take me right to it. A couple pouches of these and I'll sell my taverns and move right back to Utah and marry me a couple of wives. You sure you can find this place again?"

"Quite sure," said Crow.

A woman with a hook nose and a slender figure packed into a too-tight dress approached them. "So, boys, have you considered my offer?"

At most any other place in San Francisco this might have been considered a proposition, but the Bella Union was a respectable place—or relatively so. Out and out prostitution was not tolerated by the owner, though behind the curtained partitions he did encourage his girls to do whatever it took to sell drinks, and this might include flirtation and kisses, which most churchgoing folk would consider an unseemly way to sell your product, but then there weren't many churchgoing folk in San Francisco.

Rockwell handed Elsie the diamond. "This is worth far more than the fifteen dollars you requested to do the job, but you'll have to figure out how to divide the spoils with Charlotte."

Elsie was used to accepting payment in paper, coin, nugget or gold dust, but she goggled at the sparkling stone. "Is this a real diamond? It looks like a star fallen from the night sky!"

"Mars," said Crow.

Elsie gave him a sideways glance and she pushed the diamond inside her bodice. "Do you have the knockout drops?"

Rockwell handed over the small vial of chloral hydrate and Elsie slipped this into her bosom as well, even while brushing away a stray lock of mud-brown hair. "I'll get Charlotte right onto the job."

Elsie went over to the bar and caught the attention of a buxom house girl in a beer-stained skirt, and passed her the vial of knockout drops. With a sleight of hand that indicated that perhaps Charlotte had once worked in less reputable taverns and dance halls, those which made a practice of dosing their customers and robbing them when they slipped into unconsciousness, she shook a couple drops of chloral hydrate into one of the glasses, then made the vial disappear into the sash at her waist.

Then Charlotte climbed a curving staircase to the curtained balcony boxes, some of which were thrown open so as to enjoy the pianist and chanteuse and others that were drawn tight for privacy. Crow and Rockwell watched as she traveled halfway down the length of the balcony and entered a private box near the stage.

"So that's where Brannan is hiding out," muttered Rockwell.

"His wife might be disappointed to discover that he's spending the evening with house girls and firewater."

"Oh, his wife has long since left him, for just those reasons" said Rockwell. "Now, Brannan considers himself footloose and fancy free; even though the pesky matter of a divorce has yet to be settled."

"Do you have the knockout drops?"

There was an angry roar and a cursing which for a moment rose above the volume of Sarah Armstridge's heavenly voice, and the curtain of Brannan's box shunted aside, disgorging a staggering Charlotte, who clutched at the side of her face as if she had been struck.

"It seems that Brannan has a temper," said Crow.

"He always has, but it was very tightly controlled when he was part of the flock," replied Rockwell. "Only occasionally could you see a hint of it. Since he left the church I hear he is prone to fits of rage."

"It is the kurdaitcha working inside of him," said Crow. "The dark spirit finds a man's little weaknesses and grows them into raging giants."

Rockwell watched the buxom house girl descend the stairs, clutching at the rail. "I wonder if Charlotte was able to administer the drops?"

The answer came shortly, when Charlotte visited their table, pressing a wash rag to her cheek, where her flesh had split and she was bleeding. "I gave the knockout drops to that dirty shank. I'll let you know when he passes out, and you can do with him what you like, just promise me that it will be painful."

Crow hated to think that he'd been the cause of the woman's pain. "Why did he hit you?"

"It weren't nothing to do with the knockout drops, if that's what ye were thinking," grimaced Charlotte. "It's just that I wasn't forthcoming enough with my favors for his liking."

Cigar smoke rose thick in the rafters as Sarah Armstridge continued her songs and finally finished out her set.

Through the blue haze, Elsa approached Rockwell and Crow. "Brannan can barely put one word after the other. If you want him, he's all yours but he's got three young men with him, all lusty lads that are quick with their guns. They'll be dragging Brannan along with them if you don't make your move quickly. I've told one of the gunmen that he has a female caller on the boardwalk, but you'll have to take care of the other two yourselves."

Crow tipped his hat to Elsie. "Thank you, ma'am."

A smile touched Elsie's lips. "Ma'am? Why I've scarcely run into a gold hunter so polite, let alone an Indian!"

With hands resting on the butts of their pistols, Crow and Rockwell rose and shouldered their way through the crowds and began to climb the curving staircase to the balcony. Rockwell glanced back and noticed Charlotte at the bar, still daubing at her cheek as she prepared a drink, and watching their progress with great interest. They passed by a number of curtained boxes and heard the giggles of the house girls as they enticed their customers to purchase more drinks and the bawdy responses of the patrons hidden behind the velvet folds. The cigarette smoke gathered in thick clouds at the balcony and Crow couldn't help but cough as they strode to the box.

Rockwell swept aside the curtain and saw two gunmen lounging around a beer-stained card table examining the hand of well-worn cards in front of them. A pile of coin and paper money stood at the center of the table and these two were vying for ownership. Sam Brannan occupied the third of four chairs, slumped over and his eyes bleary slits, his cards discarded on the table in front of him.

The gunmen immediately reached for their hoglegs, but Rockwell raised a pacifying hand. "Steady, hombres. We're just here to collect Sam and take him home to sleep off his over-indulgence."

The gunman with the cleft chin and clean-shaven face narrowed one eye. He didn't draw his gun, but neither did his hand leave the polished butt of his pistol. "Who are you, Mister? We're not letting a couple of strangers haul off Brannan…and one an Indian, to boot."

"Heh," rejoined the other, tipping back his ten-gallon hat. "We might find Brannan in the alley out back, missing his scalp. Now get lost, we're in the middle of a game and we'll take Brannan home when we're good and ready or better yet we'll find a pretty little barmaid to take care of him until morning."

Seeing that he wasn't going to persuade the two, and not having the patience for any further talk, Rockwell pulled his Colt Dragoon. "Just keep your seats and continue your game, hombres. Put both hands above the table where I can see them and no one will get themselves shot."

The fingers on Ten-Gallon's gun hand twitched and in an instant Crow's gun was out and pointed at the gunman's chest. Ten-Gallon gasped when he saw how quick the Indian had made the draw.

"Listen to the man and put your hands on the table, now," said Crow. His voice was steady as though he were giving someone directions to Picnic Rock, but the Colt .45 in his grip lent menace to his words.

Ten-Gallon and the gunman with a cleft chin carefully laid their hands face-down upon the table, for they were still intent on finishing their card game when they had the chance.

The man with the cleft chin regarded the bearded intruder with a poison stare. "Wait, I know you! You're Porter Rockwell!"

"The name's Brown," growled Rockwell, but he knew his guise of anonymity had been pierced.

The ruffian with the cleft chin gazed at him with great intensity. "No! You're that Mormon devil, Porter Rockwell. You're the one that kilt my father!"

"I ain't never killed anyone that didn't need killing," said Rockwell. "Whether I killed your father or not, I can't say. Was he one of the mobocrats that was looting the Mormon settlements and raping the Mormon women? Cause, I sent a few of them along to hell."

"Ah, so you don't deny that you are Porter Rockwell!"

"And you don't deny your father was among those mobocrats," replied Rockwell.

"He was part of a twelve man peace delegation sent across the Missouri River, and you sank the barge they were on and drowned my father and eight others!"

While Rockwell kept the argument going Crow slipped forward to the chair where Sam Brannan was slumped in a barely conscious stupor. He could feel the malevolent presence of the kurdaitcha inside of him, for palpable emanations of evil beat upon him like waves upon a desolate shore. Since the kurdaitcha had taken upon her the limits of Brannan's fleshy body, her perceptions were muted and fogged by the knockout drops as well, and so Crow was able to crouch down and hoist Brannan over his shoulders, though spasms of nausea rippled through him at the contact with the former Mormon's possessed frame.

"Take their guns," said Crow.

"You don't know who you're fooling with," said Ten-Gallon. "We're part of a secret society, and when one of us is struck down vengeance is poured out upon the one who dared lift a hand against us."

"You wouldn't be speaking of the select group chosen by Sam Brannan and drawn from within Vigilance Committee?" asked Crow.

Ten-Gallon and the vigilante with the cleft chin glanced at each other.

"What do you know of it?" asked Ten-Gallon.

"Not such a secret after all, is it?" chortled Rockwell.

"Your leader is possessed by a devil," said Crow.

"She is no devil!" said Ten-Gallon. "She is the ancient power of the ages guiding us to ..." He abruptly shut his mouth when the vigilante with the cleft chin shot him a hard glance. "I don't know what you're talking about."

"Sure you don't." With Brannan slung securely over Crow's shoulders, Rockwell leaned forward to pluck the pistol from the holster of the man with the cleft chin. "It seems to me you've already made up your mind that I killed your father, but just so the record's straight, that weren't no peace delegation that your father was on. He and his murderous friends drove my people out of Illinois in the dead of winter by axe, sword, and bullet and then crossed the river after them demanding they sign legal documents ceding their abandoned properties. And when that barge sank on the way back it was God's doing ... not mine. I can't take credit for what the hand of God done."

Rockwell's hand was just about on the butt of the pistol when footsteps came stomping down the boards of the balcony with a shrill voice preceding it. "Where is that wench that told me there was a girl waiting for me in the street? There's nobody there but a street harlot..." The returning gunman broke off when he saw Sam Brannan upon Crow's shoulders, and Rockwell holding his other two friends at the point of his swept-back Dragoon pistol.

Quick as a drop of oil dancing on a hot skillet he went for his own revolver. He was faster than Rockwell and fired two bullets into his chest, so that the bearded Mormon staggered backward in the box, reeling around in a circle. Rockwell swung his own gun on the newcomer and returned as good as he got, even as he fell to the floor. The bullets punched through the gunman's chest and he reeled backward, breaking through the baluster and plunging twenty feet to land amidst a card game. The table buckled beneath his weight, scattering coin and card across the tobacco-stained boards. Sarah Armstridge ceased her song and let out a piercing scream, even while her pianist partner dove behind his piano.

Ten-Gallon reached for his pistol, but as he pulled it from his holster, Crow brought down his tomahawk and cut off the man's hand at the wrist. The spasming hand still clutched the six-shooter as it twitched on the table, pulling the trigger once so that a bullet spat past Crow and cracked a high window in the Belle Union.

The gunman with the cleft chin rolled from his seat and came up firing, but his shots were hasty and they splintered the planks around Rockwell and took off the leg of a chair, so that it toppled over on top of the Mormon. Rockwell ignored the weight of the chair and fired even as Crow wrenched his tomahawk from the face of the table and hurled it side-armed so that it imbedded in the chest of the gunman with the cleft chin.

With two bullets and a tomahawk in his chest the Missourian gave up the ghost and slumped against the pillar of the private box, blood gushing down his vest and two black bullet holes still smoking where they struck. Black powder mingled with the tobacco smoke and Crow reeled awkwardly beneath Brannan's weight as he found his footing after making the throw that had helped slay the Missouri gunman.

Rockwell stood up with a groan and shook his duster. Two bullets clattered to the floor. This hadn't been the first time that Crow had seen Rockwell take direct hits and scatter the spent lead from clothing as though they were droplets of rain from an oiled slicker. Rockwell, it seemed, never suffered more than the ill effects of bruised and battered flesh from the impact of the bullets.

The long-haired Mormon grinned at Crow. "You've probably got the only gun that can touch me, unless of course someone sheared my locks."

"I wouldn't speak that too loudly," said Crow, "unless some Delilah overhear you and get an idea in her head to turn you over to those mobocrats that dislike you so much."

Rockwell made his way to the broken railing and peered down at the dead gunman lying amidst a flurry of cardsharps attempting to recover their wagers. Some of the patrons of the Belle Union saw him and scattered. Others forgot about their own well-being and stared in awe at the perpetrator of the killing which had happened in front of their very own eyes. Such things were all too common in frontier San Francisco, but the patrons of the Belle Union were not so jaded as to be inured to a gunfight which had taken place within their earshot and their own vision.

"Let's light out of here before the constables poke their noses into the affair," said Rockwell, but Crow was already moving along the balcony and toward the descending stairs. With Brannan's weight upon his shoulders he moved deliberately so as not to take a tumble down those steps, and it took Rockwell but a few moments to catch up, slip past him and clear the way of any gawkers who might impede their progress.

Rockwell's drawn gun discouraged anybody else from getting involved and, one block away, Crow heaved Brannan's slack weight into the back of a waiting cart. They dared not leave a cart and horse unattended in even the better districts of San Francisco, for unwatched possessions disappeared faster than dew on a hot morning. The driver they had hired gave them a gap-toothed grin.

"You gentlemen seem to have kicked up a row."

"More than we would have liked," admitted Rockwell as he pulled himself up to the buckboard. "Now pony up, Sexton, before we're all gone up the flume."

Glad to have divested himself of Brannan's weight and his touch, which inspired a great depression upon his soul, Crow climbed into the back of the cart even as the driver snapped the reins and sent it barreling down the pot-holed road.

Brannan mumbled something just loud enough for Crow to hear over the rumble of the wheels and the clip of the horse's hooves. "You won't get away with this. The devil inside of me, she knows. She knows you, Demon Hunter, Priesthood Bearer, Slayer of Dark Souls. She knows you, Flapping Crow, Last of Your Tribe, and Doomed Man, and she has hungered for your destruction. She will make you beg and scream for mercy before she roasts your soul in the pits of hell." Then the chloral hydrate seized Brannan and sank him deep into the dark abysses of unconsciousness.

Rockwell shifted on the buckboard. "What did he say?"

Crow gritted his teeth. "He's rambling, Porter...just rambling."

"Any sign of the kurdaitcha?"

"Nothing yet," said Crow. "Hopefully she's buried inside the sea of brew that Brannan's imbibed. Once linked to a human a kurdaitcha cannot easily escape, and once released from a body she must find habitation in another quickly or be banished back to those dark nether realms from which she came."

"What was the vigilante with the ten gallon hat saying about the kurdaitcha being the ancient power of the ages? What was that all about?"

Crow shrugged. "Demons and devils have been around since God created our world and some for eons longer. That they would use that pedigree to gain followers is no surprise. If I've learned one thing, people will blindly follow anyone or anything if they think that they might have something to gain from it. A power that can freeze the marrow of your enemies and make the earth shake is a strong lure to some folks."

"And the kurdaitcha has that to offer," concluded Rockwell.

"As well as utter destruction when her servants have outlived their usefulness," said Crow.

Sexton guided the cart through a sharp turn. "What's this kurdaitcha thing that you two are babbling about?"

"Pull over here and let yourself out," said Rockwell. "What we're doing is dangerous, and you've already done the job we asked of you. There's no point in you taking any further risk."

Sexton grinned. "I'm not getting off this cart until you've paid me the five dollars you promised me."

Rockwell counted out five silver dollars. "I've got your money here, Sexton."

Sexton continued on for another block and then reined in his horse so that the cart came to a squealing halt. His hand dipped beneath his poncho and when it came out it held a pitted Colt Navy .36 caliber pistol.

"Gentlemen, it is with great regret that I must inform you that I have received a more lucrative offer. It seems that a group of Missourians have put up a pot of five hundred dollars as a bounty on one Porter Rockwell's head, and as much as I like you, Brown, or Porter, or whatever you call yourself, money must trump friendship. I've got soiled doves to keep in finery and furs."

"How long have we been friends, Sexton?" asked Rockwell.

"About a year," answered the gap-toothed driver. "But don't make this any harder than it has to be. It ain't nothing personal, and besides I've been friends with a man named Brown. This Porter Rockwell fellow don't mean nothing to me, and so it's easy to sell out a man I don't know."

Rockwell glanced into the darkness. "Listen, Sexton, it's very important that we get Brannan somewhere secluded. You drive us on out of here and Crow will pay you that five hundred dollars in diamonds and you won't have to split it with anyone."

"What makes you think I have partners in this?" asked Sexton. "You don't think I've got enough sense between my ears to hatch a plan like this all by myself?"

"No offense, Sexton, but no," replied Rockwell. "And when I asked you to pull over you kept going and pulled into this deserted intersection. My guess is that you've got an accomplice or two hidden away in the shadows."

"Or five," said Sexton. "I always said you were a smarter man than people gave you credit for."

"Thanks," replied Rockwell to the dubious compliment. "Now, do we have a deal or is this going down the hard way?"

"As much as I like the sound of a handful of diamonds, I don't really believe your Indian friend can get his hands on that much sparkly stone or else he'd be living in a mansion full of fountains and fine pieces of calico. I'm going to have to go with the bird in the hand ... rather than the bird in the bush. And Brown, or should I say Porter Rockwell, you're the bird in hand."

Crow reacted so swiftly that the eye could scarcely follow his hand. He drew his eagle-butted Peacemaker and fired in one motion. The bullet burst Sexton's heart and he lurched up and over the front of the cart, falling stone dead between the rear hooves of the horse and the front wheels of the cart. The horse let out a shrill cry and jerked to one side, so that the entire cart shifted and the axles groaned, complaining at the sideways pressure.

Rockwell leaned over and grabbed the reins, snapping them hard and bellowing a harsh cry. The horse responded and leaped forward, the cart nearly catapulting Crow out the back as it careened over Sexton's dead body. Even as they attempted an escape, a volley of rifle fire echoed and gun blazes painted the siding of the nearby buildings. Sexton had not lied when he claimed he had accomplices in his attempt to collect the bounty on Rockwell's head. A couple of bullets splintered the walls of the cart, but most were targeting the horse so that Rockwell could not effect their escape.

The horse screamed and reared as four separate bullets struck it. It went down thrashing, snapping one of the tether poles. In the pains of death the horse kicked off the front wheel and upset the buckboard and sent Crow and Rockwell tumbling to the street. The unconscious body of Sam Brannan flopped in the mud at Crow's booted feet, and recovering their balance Crow and Rockwell poured a barrage of lead into the dark recesses of the alley, where the position of the bounty hunters was revealed by the muzzle flash of their own gunfire, which lit up the squalid alleys and the drifting clouds of gun smoke which hazed the air. There were two gunmen on Crow and Rockwell's exposed side, but Indian and Mormon were protected somewhat from the gunfire of the three bounty hunters on the opposite side of the street by the tilted buckboard, which absorbed some of the bullets being thrown at them.

As splinters, cast up by the bullets of that trio of gunmen at their back, fogged the air around them, Crow and Rockwell targeted a rifleman crouched in the alley. They had the advantage of carrying six-shooters, where the rifleman had to load a new cartridge between each shot. Rockwell's dragon-shaped Colt Dragoon and Crow's eagle-carved Peacemaker ended the life of one of the riflemen with a half dozen bullets.

Rockwell carried a second Dragoon at his belt beneath his duster and he drew it and began firing at a rifleman hidden upon the rooftop, striking the parapet inches below the concealed bounty hunter, and driving him back into the umbra clustered around the chimneys. Crow pushed the empty cartridges out of his sacred pistol—blessed by the hand of a prophet one night the dead came to life in the salty wastes—and reloaded, even while bullets continued to pound the underside of the upset buckboard. Up to this point it had done a nice job of protecting them, but some of the bullets were finding their way through at the seams between the planks.

In all reality, even though Rockwell had temporarily caused the retreat of the gunman on the roof, they were still pinned in place. If they concentrated their fire upon the three riflemen at their back, the bounty hunter on the roof would surely creep back and fire upon them while they were turned.

"I'll fire upon the gunmen behind us," said Crow. "You kill the man on the roof when he pops his head back up."

This, of course, was easier planned than accomplished, but both Crow and Rockwell were gunmen of renowned skill and reputation. Rockwell kept the barrel of his Dragoon pistol up and trained toward the rooftop while Crow crawled around the edge of the cart and methodically fired into the dark spaces between the buildings which were briefly marked by muzzle flash. As soon as a flare of gunfire appeared he shifted his aim and snapped off two shots. He was rewarded by the sight of a bounty hunter staggering out of the shadows and falling flat on his face.

A bullet took off the spoke of the wagon wheel over Crow's head, and started it spinning. The Indian ducked back into cover even as a second rifleman sent a bullet singing past, so close that it notched the brim of Crow's hat. Now Crow noticed that Brannan was lying face down in the mud, he reached out and rolled Brannan over and noticed that no breath rose from his chest. He had suffocated in the mud, unable to lift himself out of the mire.

"Uh oh," muttered Crow.

"Uh oh, what?" demanded Rockwell. "What could be more 'uh oh' than getting caught in the crossfire of an ambush?"

"Brannan's not breathing."

"Not breathing? But doesn't that mean that the kurdaitcha is released to go into someone else's bo ..."

Rockwell broke off as a sinister force departed Brannan's body, buffeting them with waves of despair and sickness. The sensations were so strong that Crow and Rockwell were forced back against the underside of the buckboard, gasping and flailing as the dark winds of destruction attempted to enter them but, finding the vessels of their bodies inhospitable because of the holy seed of priesthood within, the kurdaitcha passed over them in search of a more easily inhabited body.

Suddenly a decidedly unmasculine cackle broke from the lips of the rifleman upon the rooftop and casting a radiation of malignant energies, which Crow and Rockwell could see and feel, he strode into sight, casting off the rifle with disdain.

"The two of you should be dead," mouthed the kurdaitcha through the bounty hunter's lips. "You've been a most persistent nuisance, and because of you I've lost an effective host. This pitiful vessel that I inhabit now has

JOEL JENKINS

no standing or wealth to help bring about my plans."

Rockwell didn't wait to find out just what the kurdaitcha's plans were; instead he thumbed back the hammer of his Dragoon and fired. The kurdaitcha gestured and the bullet froze and broke into tiny fragments before it reached her, so that the bounty hunter she inhabited was pelted with a spray of lead dust.

She laughed. "Your mortal weapons cannot harm me, Porter Rockwell."

"You know my name?" croaked Rockwell.

A dark angel formed from the unholy aura that radiated from the bounty hunter, and it was the form of a woman with flowing curves and spectral wings, whose visage alternated between one of great beauty and the aspect of a grinning skull. This body of demonic energies stayed above the bounty hunter, tethered to his physical presence. "I know you, because you were a thorn in Sam Brannan's side, a threat to his wealth which I planned to turn to my own purposes."

Seeing the manifestation of this supernatural entity, the remaining bounty hunters turned to flee down the umbra of the alleyways, but the dark angel waved a taloned hand and the blood in their veins began to ice, so that they stumbled to the ground. Even now, Crow could feel a chill growing in the air. Frost formed along the muddy street, creeping toward him and Rockwell. No talisman or coin would save them from being frozen this time, for the kurdaitcha had fixed her ill gaze upon the two of them and was intent on causing their utter destruction.

The chill seeped into Crow's limbs and his renowned lightning speed was reduced to a sluggish rise of his gun barrel as he used every bit of concentration to marshal and employ the muscles in his gun-arm, which mightily resisted his best efforts. Finally the sights were lined up and Crow pulled the trigger of his blessed Colt Peacemaker. With disdain, the kurdaitcha waved a spectral hand at the bullet, but the bullet from the blessed gun was not affected and it sped true, finding the chest of the bounty hunter upon the roof.

Immediately, the bounty hunter's knees buckled beneath him and he pitched over the parapet. He struck the ground face first, snapping his neck but still the life lingered in him and the kurdaitcha was not detached from the physical vessel of the bounty hunter to which she was tethered until the last pulse of the heart ceased. Great rage and demonic hatred emanated from the manifestation of the kurdaitcha and she howled in anger.

"As soon as he dies I will possess your body, Lone Crow and I will peer into your mind and hunt down and slay every one that you have ever loved!"

"Your mortal weapons cannot harm me, Porter Rockwell."

"Every one I've ever loved is already dead," replied Crow, but even as he said these words he realized that they were not entirely true, for there were a few he loved that yet lived.

"Then I'll hunt down every one that has ever done you a kindness and they will die horribly ... that I promise!" raged the kurdaitcha.

"Empty promises," said Crow. "You've attempted to possess both my body and Rockwell's body and been rebuffed. What makes you think that this time you will succeed?"

The dark manifestation raised a taloned hand and closed it into a fist. "Because my anger will give me strength to obliterate your accursed protections!"

Rockwell tore his eyes away from the horrible sight of the kurdaitcha who began cursing and howling. "We're minutes away from the bay, Crow. We can drag the bounty hunter's body out into the water, far enough away from any living human that she hasn't the power to possess anyone. The roar of the ocean will help drown out sound, so she will not be able to travel far."

Crow pondered this course of action for just a moment. "We won't have the time. She'll slay us with the cold before we can ever reach the bay."

The air grew icy and heavy and the mud beneath their boots froze into ice. Crow could feel the chill seeping into his bones and he could see ice crystals forming in Rockwell's thick beard. The earth began to tremble and shake, splitting the ice, which had just formed, asunder—the hollow sound of the rending echoing in their ears.

Crow knew of only one way to temporarily abate the power of the kurdaitcha and that was to slay her host. He steadied himself against the upturned buckboard and fired, putting a second bullet into the bounty hunter's broken body. This bullet finished the bounty hunter's tenuous hold upon life, breaking the kurdaitcha's tether with the body, and the fuliginous apparition of the kurdaitcha rushed upon them yet again, buffeting and bruising their bodies and seeking to enter any crevice or weakness. Rockwell stumbled over Brannan's body, falling heavily upon him as the assault continued, but when finally the kurdaitcha realized that she would not be able to gain entrance she rushed away, for her time was limited and she must find a physical form to inhabit or shortly be banished to the nether realms from which she had once been summoned.

Rockwell climbed from his knees, gasping, and Crow was in little better shape. His dark hair hung in lank strands and he felt utter exhaustion from the kurdaitcha's attack. A bit of warmth was returning to the air and the ice beginning to melt, droplets of moisture appearing in Rockwell's beard.

"Where did she go?" asked Rockwell.

"We're in the middle of a city," said Crow. "There are plenty of people within the sound of her scream, which might have been possessed."

"So how do we find her?"

"We don't," said Crow. "We could knock on hundreds of doors and never encounter her."

Rockwell crouched over Sam Brannan's quiet form, the ice flaking off his body. "So at best we've set the kurdaitcha's plans back a couple of years."

"Maybe," said Crow, "but I don't think this kurdaitcha is one to lightly give up a grudge. We've made her very, very angry."

"Nothing like a ticked off kurdaitcha riding your heels," said Rockwell. "Maybe it's time I get out of San Francisco and retreat to friendlier climes."

"Perhaps we shouldn't make ourselves so difficult to find," suggested Crow.

"You courting death, Crow?" Rockwell put his fingers just above Brannan's lips and felt the whisper of a breath. "Brannan's breathing again. My fall on him must have restarted his heart."

"Better to meet the kurdaitcha on our own terms than never knowing when she'll catch up to us," said Crow.

"I suppose," said Rockwell, but he didn't appear to be convinced. "How is meeting the kurdaitcha on our own terms do us any good if we've got nothing that can kill her? You've got your blessed gun that can kill her host body, but it didn't do nothing to the spirit inside except maybe make her angry. And she turns my bullets to snow flakes before they hit her. What good can I do except get frozen into a dad-blasted snowman?"

"First she'll use her powers of persuasion to bring humans against us," said Crow, "and you and I can fight humans. If that fails she will attempt to use her mastery over the element of cold to destroy us, and when she does we will be ready."

Rockwell shook his head. "So where are we going to set up our last stand?"

Crow didn't deny that it might well indeed be their last stand. "The same place where I believe she was summoned into this world. It sits on a ley-line and much corrupt magic was performed there, so I believe she will be drawn to it."

"Corrupt magic?" repeated Rockwell. "I don't much like the sound of that."

"Nor do I, but you've already been doing business in close proximity to

Murderer's Bar. Leave word around San Francisco that Brown is returning
to tend his bar at Middle Fork. Our kurdaitcha should have no difficulties
picking up our trail."

Sam Brannan's eyes flickered open and he shivered, clutching at the
melting frost that glittered on his arms. "I am so cold."

Rockwell wasn't too sympathetic. "You're lucky to be alive at all you
four-flushing sack of steer chips."

"What happened to me?"

"You don't remember any of it?" asked Rockwell.

"No. No … not really," answered Brannan, but there was a furtive look
in his eye.

"I think you remember it well enough," said Crow. "Now, just what was
you and what was done under the influence of the devil I don't know."

"She … she forced me to do horrible things," said Brannan.

"Ah," said Rockwell. "I see that your memory is returning. Maybe,
now that I've got your attention, you can tell me what you did with that
fifteen thousand dollars worth of tithing gold that you collected from the
California saints."

"M-most of its gone," admitted Brannan. "I bought a piece of property
in Saratoga; a vineyard, or it will be."

Rockwell scowled. "Just how much of the tithing have you got left?"

"Just the gold dust and nuggets I've got left in the pouch in my jacket."

Rockwell reached inside Brannan's jacket and extricated a one-shot
Derringer pistol scarcely as big as his palm, and then found the pouch to
which Brannan was referring. He opened it up and in the misty moonlight
he could see the golden glint of nuggets and dust within. He hefted it in
his palm, judging its weight. "This is scarcely two-hundred dollars worth
of gold, Brannan. A far cry from the fifteen thousand that you owe the
Lord."

"It's all I've got," protested Brannan. "Don't take it from me. I'll starve!"

"May the Lord have mercy on you Brother Brannan." Rockwell drew the
string of the pouch tight and dropped it into his pocket. "I'll be returning
this to Brother Brigham so that he can see it serves the saints and builds
the temple. As for you Sam Brannan, I forgive you. Let the Lord do with
you what He will."

"I'll go hungry!" cried Brannan.

"Retire to your vineyard," said Rockwell as he and Crow started down
the street. "Live off the fruit of the vine and remember if you cross me
again that next time I won't be so merciful."

━✦━

The American River roared past Murderer's Bar as Crow and Rockwell hunkered down in the damp bunker which they had dug out of the sand and rock and framed with heavy logs they had dragged from the woods. A small fire gave them warmth at the center of the bunker, and they each had three loaded rifles or carbines leaned up against the corners of their shallow pit.

Rockwell roasted a hare over the fire, and despite the enticing scent of dinner, an unsettling foreboding niggled at the corner of his mind. "I don't much like this place, Crow. I avoided it even when I was tending my bar just yonder."

"Evil lingers here," agreed Crow. "It has seeped into even the rock and tainted the river waters. See how even the weeds that spring from the sand are pale, twisted things."

Rockwell stared down the river and at the darkness of the forest, past the trio of tar-soaked teepees that stood at the edges of Murderer's Bar. "This is the third night that we've camped in this forsaken pit we've dug. Do you really think the kurdaitcha is coming for us?"

Crow sliced a strip of meat from the roasting hare and sampled it. "I think that we've made a vengeful spirit very angry and she doesn't have the temperament to do anything but hunt us down and kill us. It's only a matter of time, Porter."

"I'm having a devil of a time trying to keep my feet dry in the mean time," said Rockwell.

As if in response to his complaint a rifle shot cracked in the darkness, flaring from the forest beyond the river's edge, and the bullet sinking into the log bordering the pit in which they crouched. Crow was leaning against the log and he could feel the tremor run through it.

He licked his fingers clean as he ducked down, wiped his hand on his trousers and reached for one of the already-loaded rifles leaning in the corner. "It seems as though we're done waiting."

"Finally," said Rockwell, who plucked up a Sharps rifle, "a target that I can vent my spleen on."

"If only we could actually see them," said Crow.

Now, a number of muzzle flashes blossomed in the night, the reports of the enemies' rifles scarcely heard over the roaring of the river.

"I'm counting seven gunmen," said Rockwell. "What have you got?"

"I've got seven as well." None of the rifle shots got any nearer than the first, but the bullets fairly skipped around their dug-out fortress, and they could hear the whine of their passing.

"Maybe we should extinguish the fire," said Rockwell. "So they have less of a target."

"We may need the fire later," said Crow. "We're going to have to risk it."

Rockwell fired a shot into the forest, in the general direction of a muzzle flash. He didn't give much for his chances of actually hitting one of the riflemen. "That's just to let them know that we're here, alive and kicking."

Crow unleashed a shot as well, but thought it just as unlikely that he might strike one of the enemy. He crouched down and took his time reloading while the enemy bullets moaned overhead. "Let them spend their ammunition. Eventually, they'll realize that they need to get closer. That's when we'll hit them."

Rockwell peered from over the lip of their makeshift palisade. "Hmph, it looks as though they're already getting impatient."

Indeed, moon-dappled figures scrambled from the woods, counting on the covering fire of their compatriots to give them safety while they advanced on Murderer's Bar. For a moment their faces lifted and Rockwell could see beneath the concealing brims of their hats. He recognized at least two of them. "It's Mad Henry Mortenson and Bloody Luke Piles; two of the nastiest blokes of Sydney Town, if ever I knowed just one of 'em."

Crow nodded. He'd all too many experiences with Sydney Town and its residents or ducks as the locals called them. It was nothing more than a penal colony which had relocated from the shores of Australia. Some of the residents had been given Tickets of Leave by British Magistrates who were more than happy to rid themselves of the nuisance of habitual criminals and thieves. Others had left the land of aborigines and kangaroos without bothering with any of the legal niceties. Once, already, firebugs from Sydney Town had burned San Francisco to the ground, just for the pleasure of watching the conflagration and warming their hands upon the flames.

"It looks as though the kurdaitcha has gathered together every murderer and cutthroat she could find in Sydney Town." Rockwell popped up, laid his rifle on the log and put a bullet through the crown of an Australian who was splashing across the shallows of the river, thinking to use the rise of the sand bar as cover. He hadn't been ducking low enough however, and a gout of blood spurted from his skull as he pitched backward and was pulled into the heavy currents of the river.

"Not every cutthroat and murderer," replied Crow. "Or we'd have hundreds coming for us."

Bloody Luke Piles disappeared from sight and into the umbra-cloaked landscape and scrub brush, reappearing from behind a stunted pine that clung to the rock and sand of the bar. He fired his rifle from the hip and struck Rockwell in his hat, so that it spun around on his head, the bullet entering through the brim, traveling around the Mormon's head, and exiting at the back of the hat.

Crow had no such invulnerability to bullets, but when Bloody Luke Piles took a shot at Rockwell it temporarily exposed him to the aim of the Indian gunslinger. Crow threw his carbine to his shoulder and fired off a quick shot that punched through Bloody Luke Piles sternum and dropped him like a sack of barley.

Rockwell righted his hat upon his head. "That's two down."

Before he finished speaking Mad Henry Mortenson came barreling out of the darkness, firing wildly with his pistol. None of his shots found their mark, though dirt and gravel sprayed from the dint of the ricocheting bullets. This did not deter Mad Henry Mortenson, however, and he launched himself into the pit, at Crow, bringing the barrel down on Crow's head.

The Indian felt the impact of the barrel as it crushed the crown of his hat, but it was a glancing blow and Crow reversed his grip on his carbine and shoved the maple wood stock into Mortenson's jaw. Though Crow heard the jaw pop out of place this did not deter Mortenson in the slightest., He struck at Crow over and over, with more ferocity than skill. Rockwell was busy firing at another Sydney Town Duck who was attempting to ford the shallows of the river, and so Crow was on his own. He managed to fend off the majority of the falling blows by raising the barrel and stock of his carbine in front of him to absorb the strikes. As the barrel of the pistol clanged against the barrel of his carbine, Crow thrust hard to gain a little space between himself and his opponent, and let go of his carbine. He reached down with his right hand and swept his tomahawk out of its sheath and the upward stroke carried the blade into the joint of Mortenson's throat where it met his dislocated jaw.

Mad Henry Mortenson fell back against the side of the pit, clutching vainly at the tomahawk lodged in his throat. He burbled out some unintelligible curses and collapsed, blood running down the front of his flannel shirt. Briefly, Crow was reminded of the desperate battles he had fought against the rebels in the Civil War. Most of those were good, if perhaps misguided men, and he had shed tears at their deaths. There was nothing good about Mad Henry Mortenson, and Crow shed no tears at his passing. Instead, he grabbed up his last loaded rifle.

"Crow!" Rockwell fired a bullet at a woman who was fording the stream and it shattered into crystalline fragments before it ever touched her body. Where her bared legs touched the water, for she had hoisted the hem of her skirt, ice floes formed, and as she rose from the river she walked upon the edges which froze solid beneath her sand-caked toes. "It's the kurdaitcha! She's inhabited the body of Eliza 'cutthroat' Feller!"

Eliza Feller was known for having cut the throat of one wealthy client while he slept, emptying his wallet, and burying his body in the stable. No one could prove it, of course, but everyone knew it to be the truth. Even as Rockwell recognized her, the face of Eliza 'cutthroat' Feller, whose body the kurdaitcha now possessed, began to ripple and transform, showing the skull-like visage of the demonic presence within. Dark waves of energy radiated, chilling Crow and Rockwell to the bone, while ice crept over Murderer's bar, encroaching on the pit where the two gunfighters had chosen to make their stand.

"How fitting," said the kurdaitcha, her voice like steel grinding against steel, "that I should find the two of you cowering at the very place where I was birthed into this world. It was here that the blood of Indian and white man mingled in a shaman's sacrifice that brought me forth from the nether dark nesses, and it is here again where the blood of white man and Indian will mingle as I cement my place of power upon the throne of this pulsing earth."

Now the cold seemed to leap upon them, rather than to creep, and their breath rose in icy particles. The kurdaitcha breathed out, and tendrils of cold whipped toward them, chill creeping into the center of their bones as the possessed prostitute approached them on frozen ground. As frost formed upon their hats and clothing, Crow and Rockwell reached for pitch-soaked brands and thrust them into the fire, so that they blazed forth with light, which refracted among the icy motes that hung heavy in the air.

Both Crow and Rockwell knew that they had only moments to act before they were subsumed by the elemental cold drawn forth by the kurdaitcha, and with ice cracking and sloughing from their clothing they tossed the brands at the tar-soaked teepees that formed a triangle around them. As soon as the flaming brands struck, they ignited the teepees and the tinder and dry wood which they had so carefully stacked inside, so that instantly three pillars of flame rose about them. The intense heat pushed against the pervading cold, melting the frost on the ground and pushing warmth into the limbs of the odd partnership of the Indian and the Mormon gunfighter.

The kurdaitcha threw up an arm to ward off the intense heat and the flaring brightness. Rockwell drew his Dragoon pistol and began to fire, hopeful that the heat might be so intense that the kurdaitcha might not be able to ward off the bullets as she had previously. The bullets lasted longer than before, and they drew within inches of piercing her skin before they shattered into shards. These shards peppered the kurdaitcha's flesh, but they did not penetrate deep enough to do more than irritate the kurdaitcha to even greater anger.

She shrieked out curses that were ancient before even the ancient of days and his wife Eve first trod the hallowed paths of Eden. She pushed out a hand and a cone of cold projected, battering Crow as he drew forth his blessed eagle-butted Colt Peacemaker. The marrow chilled within his bones. It was difficult for Crow to even wrap his hand around the butt of his pistol, and so this was far from his fastest draw; in fact, it was probably the slowest draw he'd ever made since he first strapped on a gun. Still, he managed to level his pistol and fire a bullet. It pierced Eliza Feller's upraised palm and traveled down her forearm, lodging in flesh and bone. The gun shot was not enough to slay Feller, but to a kurdaitcha the bullet from the blessed gun was as a poison.

She spat out an oath in some demonic tongue learnt from the frothing, flaccid lips of monstrous things better left unimagined and clutched her shattered arm to her bosom. With great deliberation and clumsy fingers, Crow managed to pull back the hammer of his pistol, hoar-frost still clinging to the metal despite the raging pillars of fire which formed a protective barrier around them, and he pulled the trigger again. This time the bullet pierced Eliza Feller's breast and she fell with a shriek that carried upon it the kurdaitcha's departing essence.

The kurdaitcha did not attempt, this time, to enter the bodies of Crow or Rockwell. Instead it fled across the frozen waters, to the body of a Sydney Town rifleman who drew close to the opposite shore, drawn by the spectacle of ice and flame, bullets and blood. Despite the roar of the flame and the roar of the outer river, which had not been turned to ice, he was within earshot of that scream, and the kurdiatcha rode those sonic waves into the body of the rifleman, whose body spasmed as she entered and took control.

Crow lurched to the perimeter of the flaming teepees and fired his last four shots. His aim was poor because he couldn't force his frozen limbs to respond to his mental commands as well as he was accustomed. The first two bullets pocked the ice at the shore and the third broke a stone beneath the rifleman's feet. The fourth shot, however, climbed high enough, and it penetrated the belly of the Sydney Town duck, so that he collapsed, letting go of his rifle, and clutching at his leaking belly. The wound would not be fatal for some time, and so the kurdaitcha remained tethered to the Australian criminal, her essence hovering and shifting above him as she attempted to bring her powers to bear against Crow and Rockwell.

However, as long as Crow and Rockwell stood within the perimeter formed by the flaming pillars of the burning tents, the cold could not overcome them. In fact, the fierce flame began to return warmth to their flesh, and feeling began to be restored to their numbed fingers.

"What happens when the Sydney duck finally dies?" asked Rockwell.

"The last couple of gunmen that she brought with her have fled," said Crow. "They'll be out of earshot and safe from possession well before he dies."

"I've chased everyone out of my tavern and camp … for that matter," said Rockwell. "They'd likely be out of hearing range anyway, but I didn't want to take no chances."

So, from within the safety of the triple infernos Rockwell and Crow kept a long vigil through the night until, finally, the Sydney Town duck died and the kurdaitcha let out a shriek upon which her essence burst forth, seeking for a body to inhabit. Crow and Rockwell felt themselves buffeted, as if by the very powers of Satan, himself, and for a few moments of despair they were exposed to the darkness of the kurdaitcha's soul as she attempted to claw open their minds and enter their bodies, but then she dissipated like the morning dew before the sun's rays, and fresh hope replaced despair.

Indeed, a glimmer of dawn began to paint the sky of the Eastern horizon, for their vigil had taken them through the darkest hours of night.

"Is she gone?" Rockwell hoisted himself off the earth where he had fallen.

Crow, likewise, pulled himself up from the earth where he had fallen at the terrific onslaught of the kurdaitcha. "I don't feel her presence anywhere near. Perhaps she has been banished back to the nether realms from whence she came."

"But will she stay there?" asked Rockwell.

Crow's face was taciturn. "Until some other fool mingles blood in a sacrifice to bring her forth again."

"I guess I'm going to have to face Brigham Young and tell him I've failed to bring back the tithing," said Rockwell. "The church is in sore need of those funds."

"Maybe we should go visit that diamond field I know," suggested Crow.

"It won't be the tithing money you were sent for, but those diamonds could help build that temple in Salt Lake."

Rockwell considered this for just a moment. "And this isn't some wild goose chase you're leading me on, Crow? Because I'm far too worn out to go gallivanting around California looking for some fool's dream."

"You held one of those diamonds in your hand," said Crow. "Did it feel like a dream to you?"

Rockwell laughed. "When we ride together I'm never sure whether I should be believing the things my own eyes have seen. It all seems like dream; a very, very bad one."

THE END

LONE CROW

The character of Lone Crow is one that's been fermenting in my mind for over three decades. I thought it would be interesting to cast a Native American in the role of the gunfighter—a role that's been traditionally reserved for characters of European descent. When Russ Anderson of PulpWork Press floated the idea of a weird west anthology I added another wrinkle, making Crow an occult investigator of sorts.

With these two elements in place, the adventures of Lone Crow began to explode in my brain, presenting themselves faster than I could write them. These stories have appeared in all of the How the West was Weird books, Six Guns Straight From Hell, Low Noon, Strange Trails, Gunslingers & Ghost Stories, and Showdown at Midnight. An anthology of Lone Crow stories entitled *The Coming of Crow* was published by PulpWork Press this year, as well

JOEL JENKINS - lives with his wife and children in the heron-haunted and bigfoot-bedeviled hills and forests of the Great Northwest. When not fending off feral bobcats or hirsute sasquatches, Jenkins composes weird tales by the flickering light of his hydroelectric-powered computer. For a complete listing of his various novels and collections visit JoelJenkins.net, sign up for his infrequent newsletter, and get free stuff.

THE STRIX SOCIETY

BY

JOSH REYNOLDS

"Was this the face that launch'd a thousand ships and burnt the topless towers of Ilium? Sweet Helen, make me immortal with a kiss."
-Christopher Marlowe, "Doctor Faustus", Scene XIII

"**T**he Strix Society," Lord Curzon said, without preamble. "You know of it?"

"I dare say I know something. A strix is a flesh eating night bird and a harbinger of ill-omen from Greek mythology," Charles St. Cyprian said. "And a society, well...self explanatory, what?"

"I did not come here for japes and mockery, sir," Curzon said stiffly.

"No, I expect not. Fine, yes, I have heard of them. They are very much in my line, one might say," St. Cyprian said, leaning back in his chair. He and Curzon sat across from each other in the large wingback chairs which occupied the oddly patterned Turkish rug before the sitting room's cavernous Restoration-era fireplace.

George Curzon, The Earl Curzon of Kedlestone, and Foreign Secretary to His Majesty's government, was an older man with a face like a dyspeptic eagle, who wore ill-humor-like armor. He was dressed fashionably, if slightly out of joint with current trends. For Curzon, Victorian black served for every occasion.

In contrast, St. Cyprian, almost forty years Curzon's junior, was a slim man of olive complexion dressed in one of the finest modern sartorial creations to ever leave a Seville Row tailors' shop and deign to live in man's closet. He had been preparing for an evening out, when his guest had arrived and insisted on speaking, despite the lack of appointment. Still, when the former Viceroy of India showed up at one's doorstep, demanding attention, one had best brew a cuppa and settle in for a chat.

"Your line," Curzon repeated, chewing the words. "Yes, I suppose that's right."

St. Cyprian smiled. His line, such as it was, included the investigation, organization and occasional suppression of That Which Man Was Not Meant to Know…including ghosts, werewolves, ogres, fairies, boggarts and the occasional worm of unusual size…by order of the King (or Queen), for the good of the British Empire. Such were the duties and responsibilities of the Royal Occultist.

Formed during the reign of Elizabeth the First, the office of Royal Occultist (or the Queen's Conjurer, as it had been known) had started with the diligent amateur Dr. John Dee, and passed through a succession of hands since. The list was a long one, weaving in and out of the margins of British history, and culminating in the Year of Our Lord 1920, in one Charles St. Cyprian and his erstwhile assistant-cum-apprentice, Ebe Gallowglass.

Gallowglass had already long scarped for her evening's planned debauchery when Curzon arrived. St. Cyprian had been intent on his dinner reservations at the Savoy, and the company of the young woman he'd been intending to enjoy said reservations with, when the Foreign Secretary had arrived, plainclothes policemen in tow. The latter were even now outside occupying the stoop of No. 427 Cheyne Walk, like as not flicking cigarette ash into his nasturtiums as they tried to look inconspicuous. He'd cancelled his reservation, and the date, and gotten an earful over the blower from both the maitre d' and the woman, respectively. He was trying his best not to let it color his mood, but it was a losing battle.

"I should hope so, seeing as you're here." St. Cyprian gestured airily to the sitting room around them. Pictures of former bearers of the office lined the walls of the sitting room, jostling for space with fetish masks and lurid artworks by Goya and Blake. Great bookshelves groaned beneath a library of occult works, as well as a century's worth of accumulated bric-a-brac. Over the fireplace hung a *xiphos;* a double-edged, single-handed sword with a leaf-shaped blade. It was a family heirloom, supposedly brought over with Brutus and his Trojans, and St. Cyprian had used it to good effect more than once.

"Yes," Curzon said as he looked around with a grimace. "I wouldn't be, if I had any other option, you know." He sounded as if he held St. Cyprian personally responsible.

"You'd be surprised how often people say that," St. Cyprian said.

"No, I don't think so," Curzon said.

St. Cyprian chuckled and lifted the tea pot off of the rack in the fireplace as it began to whistle. He carefully filled two cups and handed one to Curzon, who accepted it gingerly. He sniffed it and took a sip. St. Cyprian took a sip of his own and said, "So, might one inquire as to why you're here?"

"My daughter is to be married," Curzon grunted. "A fellow named Mosley."

"Congratulations." St. Cyprian knew the man in question by reputation. Oswald Mosley was the ambitious scion of Staffordshire landowners, and the youngest member to take a seat in the House of Commons. He was also, in the words of the honourable Freddie Threepwood, an absolutely perfect perisher. Given that Freddie had been kicked out of Eton and Oxford for various offenses, St. Cyprian thought he knew whereof he spoke, when he spoke of perishers, perfect or otherwise.

"He's a bounder and a cad. He's after her inheritance," Curzon said, unknowingly echoing the honourable Freddie's sentiments.

"My sympathies," St. Cyprian said smoothly.

Curzon shook his head dismissively. "What do you know about the Strix Society, St. Cyprian?" he asked.

St. Cyprian decided to take the question seriously this time. "They're fairly new, as these sorts of people go. They take their name from their president, Miss Helen Strix, late of Paris, before that Vienna, and before that Venice. She's not British, though she seems to have had little difficulty in ensconcing herself in the welcoming swirl of London's bright young things. Her society is made up of the mad, the bad, the peculiar and the crankish by all accounts. No one seems to know what they stand for, or for what purpose they gather, beyond wild parties and the like."

"Mosley has apparently been seen in their company," Curzon said. He hesitated, and then added, "They are, according to some, considering him for membership."

"You don't seem terribly worried, if you don't mind me saying so," St. Cyprian said, as he took a sip of tea.

"I do mind," Curzon said. He set his cup down. "But you are not wrong. He is hardly suitable, but Cimmie...Lady Cynthia...is besotted with the ambitious little rascal nonetheless. And if he has fallen in with...the wrong sort, I wish to know about it."

"Why not simply hire a detective, then? Plenty of that lot about, I'm given to understand. You can find them in practically every A. B. C. teashop and Piccadilly flat. I have that Blake fellow's number, if you'd like."

Curzon made a face. "That sort won't do, and you know it." His eyes were hard. "I saw...things, in my time in India and Persia. I won't pretend to understand them, but I'm not the sort of man to deny what's right in front of me. I got a sense for that sort of thing, and I feel it now." He hesitated. Then, "You've heard the stories, I trust?"

"About the society or your son-in-law to be?" St. Cyprian asked.

Curzon frowned. "About the society, dash it!" He jerked forward, and began to cough. His body shook, as St. Cyprian watched silently. Curzon didn't look well, he thought. Drained, weak, and frailer than he ought, even for a man of his years and career. Curious, he made a stealthy gesture with the fingers of his free hand to 'twang the cords invisible' as his predecessor had called it. For a brief moment, he could see the psychical miasma which clung to his guest. He had seen something similar once before, during a particularly bad case involving a child's doll house and the peculiar thing in its attic, and he shivered slightly.

"Yes," St. Cyprian said. He set his cup aside. "Hard not to, given their propensity for the night life. They're a wild lot; practically bacchanalian. There's some talk of blood-red rooms and ancient rites and all that sort of tosh, but that's not so out of bounds for such queer little clubs." He ran his hand through his hair. "I know that they're not open to applications. One must be invited to join, and sponsored. They're looking for a specific sort, these Strix Society chappies, though no one knows just what that sort might be." His lips quirked into not-quite a smile. "If your son-in-law to be has been invited, that doesn't speak well for his character, I dare say."

Curzon glowered at him for a moment, and then looked away. St. Cyprian felt a flush of pity. Curzon was a harsh man, in some ways. He was prone to defensiveness and blunt speeches, but that didn't make him a bad man. He loved his daughter that much was obvious. He pulled a silver cigarette case out of his coat pocket, opened it, took one and proffered the case to Curzon. The latter took one and St. Cyprian scraped a match against the rough edge of the table to light it for him. Then he did the same for his own.

"She loves him," Curzon said after a minute, expelling the words amidst a cloud of smoke.

"So she does," St. Cyprian said. "A good enough reason, one supposes. Have no fear, Lord Curzon. If your lad is a-straying, we shall have him back on the straight and narrow directly."

"I have no doubt. A mutual friend speaks highly of you," Curzon said. "He said you handled a rather delicate affair in Whitechapel back in

January, and that disturbance at the Voyager's Club last week. And then, of course, there was that rather nasty business in Persia, in the last year of the war." He said that last bit hesitantly. "With those...people. You recall?"

"Yes," St. Cyprian said after a moment. He felt the itch of old scars, but resisted the urge to scratch. "I was Carnacki's assistant then. One of our last cases together before..." He trailed off, and took a drag on his cigarette. Memories of that last day at Ypres, never buried far beneath the surface of his thoughts, surfaced sourly, if briefly, and for a moment, his nose was again filled with the stink of mud, blood and explosions. He blinked, banishing the memories back to their black corner and took a shudder-y breath.

"He was a good chap, was Thomas," Curzon said softly, after a moment. "He was an honest man, and I always appreciated that about him." He expelled a cloud of smoke and said, "Did he ever tell you about that business in Bombay, in 1904?"

"No," St. Cyprian said. He waited for Curzon to go on, but instead, the older man abruptly stood.

"You'll see to it then?"

St. Cyprian rose to his feet. "I will," he said simply. Curzon didn't offer to shake hands, and St. Cyprian would have been surprised if he had. He saw the Foreign Secretary out and back into the custody of his protective flock of policemen. As he closed the door on his guest, he thought about the Strix Society. What he knew was mostly rumour and innuendo, but none of it was particularly pleasant.

In the War, he'd been able to *feel* an artillery barrage before it hit. Like hearing thunder in your bones, or feeling rain in your joints. He had that same feeling now, closing in from all sides. There was a storm gathering, somewhere out there. He'd felt it for weeks, and when Curzon had come to him; he'd realized what it must be.

He'd made it a point, upon taking up his duties, that he'd only investigate where and when absolutely necessary. Previous incumbents had tried, more than once, to drive the money-changers out of the temple so to speak, but St. Cyprian had lived through a mundane war and found he had no taste for the occult variety. It was bad enough dealing with isolated practitioners whose knowledge of the invisible far out-stripped his own; going up against the Sisterhood of Rats or the Si-Fan when, by and large, they adequately policed themselves, was not something he looked forward to. If Scotland Yard could look the other way, so could he. If some bunch of amateur, fifth form demonologists in Surrey wanted to summon Mephistopheles without considering the consequences, on their heads be it.

But sometimes…sometimes it spilled over. Sometimes the Devil's rain fell on the unjust and the just alike. And that was where the Royal Occultist came in. In a way, Curzon had given him the excuse he needed to poke and pry into what was otherwise none of his business.

"Lucky me," he murmured. As the words left his mouth, he heard the scuff of a worn down shoe on the floor behind him. He spun, and found himself looking down the barrel of a Webley-Fosbery revolver. He swatted the barrel of the pistol aside and snapped, "Oh put it away, would you? I'm in no mood for your games."

Ebe Gallowglass grinned like a cat who had just fallen into a vat of cream and stowed her pistol in the holster hanging beneath her arm. She was dark and thin and slightly feral looking, with black hair cut in a razor-edged bob, and a battered man's flat cap resting high on her head. She wore a man's clothes as well, beneath her convoy coat. "So, who was that then?" she asked, as she took off the latter.

"Lord Curzon, if you can believe it," he said.

"Cor, really?" she said. Then, "Who's Lord Curzon?"

St. Cyprian stared at her for a moment, and then shook his head slowly. "Someone who's asked us to look into something. You're back early, by the by. And distinctly unspifflicated." He detected a draft, and knew she'd come in by the back door and, as usual, not bothered to close it.

"So are you," she retorted.

"Never went out, more like." St. Cyprian frowned. "But I intend to rectify that." He smiled at her and extended his elbow. "Care to accompany me?"

She glowered at him. "I just got back."

He lowered his arm. "Fine. Stay here. Don't touch the gin in the cabinet. That's for guests. And it's expensive. I won't have you guzzling it like you did the brandy."

"I'm a guest. And what did that Curzon bloke want?" she asked, following him back into the sitting room.

He stubbed out his still smoldering cigarette and picked up his coat from where he'd tossed it. "You've been squatting in the second bedroom for a year now; you're a tenant, not a guest. And he wants me…"

"Us," Gallowglass interjected.

St. Cyprian looked at her, a half-smile on his face. "Decided to accompany me then, Miss Gallowglass?"

"Someone has to make sure you don't get coshed in an alley, don't they?"

she said, pulling on her coat. "Finish what you were saying."

"Lord Curzon asked that we look into the doings of the Strix Society. And since my evening schedule is now clear, we might as well make a go of it soonest, what?" He slipped on his coat and headed for the door. Gallowglass hurried after him.

"Where are we going, then?"

"To see about wrangling an invitation, of course. We'll take the Crossley."

The black Crossley 20/25 had carried them from one end of the country to the other, at various times. The car was the same make and model used by the Flying Squad of the London Metropolitan Police and had been, at various times, crushed, burned, submerged, frozen and dropped from an impressive height. Nonetheless, it continued to trundle on as dutifully as the day he'd bought it, give or take a dent or six.

The night wasn't especially pleasant. The canvas roof wobbled and rustled with a steady drizzle of rain, and thin squirming of water poured down the windscreen. St. Cyprian hunched forward in the driver's seat, peering ahead at the houses to either side of the street as they headed deeper into darkest Westminster. As he related what Curzon had told him to Gallowglass, he aimed the car towards the West End and Piccadilly Circus.

He knew little else regarding the Strix Society than what he'd shared with Curzon. But what he did know was that they'd made the bawdier bits of the West End their hunting ground for the past few weeks, shifting themselves from one soiree and bottle party to the next like a school of social piranha. "Helen Strix," he said, finally.

"What's that when it's at home?" Gallowglass sat slumped in her seat, arms crossed, head bowed, and feet pressed to the windscreen.

"What do you know about her?" he asked sternly.

Gallowglass sucked on her teeth for a moment and then said, "Foreign, ain't she? Got money though. Supposed to be a knockout, innit?"

"So one hears," he said, pleased. In their line, it paid to know who was getting up to what sort of mischief where and when. Normally, such things held little interest for his assistant. But for once, she'd been paying attention. There might be some hope for her yet.

Some Royal Occultists retired, but most died. By accident or by design, they died and were replaced by royal edict, like stripped out cogs plucked from a machine, lest they damage the mechanism. Given that such was the case, it made sense to have the next cog standing by, ready to be slotted in. Gallowglass, however, still had quite a ways to go before she was fit for purpose. She was far too inclined to unlimber the artillery for his taste; while shooting things was sometimes the way of it, there were other times where *not* shooting something was equally important. Until she figured out which was which, he supposed he would have to try and not get killed.

"She's rarely seen out and about," he continued. "But the society that's taken her name have been all too visible lately. They've swooped down on every party and shindig that's worth the name, leeching guests and reputedly taking them back to a house in Seven Dials for a proper knees-up, hosted by the Strix Society."

"Why?"

"No bloody idea," he said cheerfully. "I suspect we shall find out directly, what?" He gestured to the windshield, where the rain-blurred reflections of the electric signs of Piccadilly Circus where visible. Incandescent light bulbs flickered and steamed in the rain as they struggled to illuminate the benefits of Bovril and Schweppes Ginger Ale to passers-by below. Loud music and raucous laughter floated on the damp air, echoing into Shaftesbury Avenue and Coventry Street from the well-lit interiors of nightclubs. The streets were crowded, despite the rain, as lorries, automobiles and omnibuses caught the curve of the roundabout and perambulated through the circuitous confines of the Circus. The pavement too was packed with pedestrians, hurrying here and there, seeking shelter from the weather in nightclubs, theatres and pubs.

St. Cyprian guided the Crossley onto Coventry Street, and parked near the J. Lyons and Co. Corner House. Gallowglass swung her feet down and sat up. "Where to now?"

"Where the music is the loudest and the crowd drunkest, I should think." He pulled up the collar of his battered 'British Warm,' an officer's greatcoat, and swung out into the rain. Gallowglass followed him.

"How will we recognize them?" she asked, hurrying after him, her shoulders hunched against the chill. "Not like they're wearing signs."

"Oh, they're easy enough to spot," he said. "They have a fondness for red, and in garish quantities. We see a flock of red, we cast our net."

"And just how are we going to get an invitation to one of these parties of theirs?"

"That, I'm afraid, we'll have to figure out on the fly." He stopped and looked at her. "It may take several nights worth of carousing, I fear. Are you up to it?"

"Sounds like berries to me," she said, grinning.

"I rather thought it might."

For the next few hours, they wandered from nightclub to bottle party, moving through a sea of bright young things engaged in enthusiastic excess, eyes peeled for a splash of red in the sea of furs, dinner jackets and baggy trousers. Alcohol flowed freely, and group of fancy dress revelers stumbled through traffic on scavenger hunts. Several times he ran into familiar faces, staggering along. It was said that if one stayed in Piccadilly Circus long enough, one would eventually bump into everyone one knew.

For St. Cyprian it was familiar territory. In the months after the War, he'd tried to lose himself in the welcoming haze of parties and drink. He'd snatched policemen's helmets with the Wooster crowd and gone swimming in the Trafalgar fountains with the Runcible set. He hadn't quite put all of that behind him...he still enjoyed the occasional bout of auto-polo...but he'd come to see it for what it was. The parties, the indulgence, all of it was an attempt to forget how close things had come to tipping over entirely during the war. God alone knew what would happen if there were another blow-up.

He forced the thought aside as the clock face above the Saqui & Lawrence across the street struck midnight. The rain had stopped at last, and neon puddles covered the bumpy surface of the street. Gallowglass had pinched a bottle of something from somewhere and swigging it down with gusto.

A flash of red caught his eye, and he felt a familiar rumble in his bones. He sought out the red dress, too bright, too vibrant to be entirely fashionable, as it weaved through the crowd around the statue of Eros on its fountain-plinth, and started after it. "I do believe that the game's afoot, Miss Gallowglass," he said, as she fell into step beside him.

"How can you tell?" she asked, slapping the nearly empty bottle into the hands of a startled pedestrian.

"The nose knows," he said, tapping his.

"Knows what? She smells bad?"

"It was a figure of speech," St. Cyprian said. They crossed the street amidst a flurry of horns, using a crowd of party-goers for cover. "I've got a sense for these things, you know." Gallowglass' reply was inelegant and unladylike. As they reached the fountain, St. Cyprian hopped up onto it to get a better view of his surroundings. He caught sight of the red dress again, as it made its way towards Regent Street and the boarded over windows of Swan & Edgar Ltd. The department store had been hit in the last zeppelin raid of 1917, and had been closed to the public ever since. As he watched, the boards were moved aside and a small crowd of people began to filter in, their trespass unobserved in the general hubbub of the evening. "There!" he said, hopping down.

He and Gallowglass hurried in pursuit of their quarry. As they reached the boarded over storefront, St. Cyprian caught the strain of music coming from within. Gallowglass pried one of the boards away, and slithered inside before St. Cyprian could caution her. He squirmed after her, cursing under his breath as his overcoat caught on the boards.

Even nearly three years after the fact, the inside of the store still stank of the fire that had erupted after it had been struck by enemy ordinance. It was in the midst of a long overdue refurbishment, the display counters were empty and the walls still caked with ash. The music echoed out of the rear of the store, and they followed it behind a heavy curtain and into a large room, packed with party-goers. A display case had been pressed into service as a bar, and a stage had been improvised from scaffolding and tarpaulin. A band was hard at it, playing something boisterous and American, as the party-goers danced with less rhythm than enthusiasm.

St. Cyprian let his gaze roam across the crowded room. Men and women in red circulated like blood vessels through the crowd, mingling in ad hoc fashion. More display cases had made over into temporary tables, and everything was lit by a combination of candles and electric lanterns. Under other circumstances, he might have taken a table and settled in to enjoy himself. "What I want to know is why they wear red," Gallowglass muttered as she looked around.

"Certain colors have certain significances," he said. As he scanned the room, he saw a familiar face. "We're in luck," he said. "Mosley is here tonight. Over there, in the red waistcoat." He gestured surreptitiously towards a tall, thin young man near the stage who was leaning over a makeshift table, speaking quietly to a giggling trio of young women.

Mosley looked like a well-fed fox; sleek and smooth. His hair was slicked back tight to his skull and his moustache quirked pompously at the ends. He wore evening wear, and the only dash of color was his waistcoat. As St. Cyprian watched, Mosley smoothed his moustache with the tip of a finger, in a gesture he probably thought was rather dashing, but which, from a distance, merely looked vulgar.

"Who...the git with the curly mustache?" Gallowglass said. "He's not wearing all red."

"Yes, quite," St. Cyprian said. "And Curzon said he wasn't a member yet." He glanced around, noting others who bore similar splashes of crimson like the proverbial mark of Cain moving here and there through

"What I want to know is why they wear red?"

the crowd. "Maybe this is an initiation of some kind..." he trailed off and shook his head, "No matter. Our course is clear."

"Right. We planning to snatch him?"

"No. Tonight is about the soft approach, I think. I get Mosley alone, and have a quiet chat. Who knows, he might be a reasonable sort. He is an ambitious little peacock. If I put the risk of his current associations to him plain enough, he may well cut ties voluntarily."

Gallowglass snorted. "Be a bloody wonder," she muttered.

"Cynicism does not become you, Miss Gallowglass."

"And what if he likes his new friends just fine?" she asked as they began to make their way through the crowd. "If this is an initiation, he might not be keen on cutting it short."

"We'll cross that bridge if we should come to it. If this can be resolved without causing an incident, so much the better. Now, go hobnob and try not to cause a scene. I need you to keep an eye on Mosley's crimson-clad companions, what? Make sure no one takes an undue interest in our confab, what?"

"I'll have you know I can hob with the best of nobs," she said. She tossed off a two-fingered salute and eeled her way into the crowd. There was enough fancy dress on display that he wasn't worried about her standing out too much, if anyone noticed her, which he doubted. Gallowglass was a master of the art of the unobtrusive sidle, and a champion creeper. She was practically an alley cat in a flat cap.

He looked around the room and his senses, both physical and otherwise, reached out, taking the pulse of the crowd and the building both as he moved in a roundabout way towards Mosley. There was a pall over everything and he was put in mind of what a hare must feel, as the fox closes in. Something was coming, something vast and terrible and he had no idea where it was coming from or what form it would take and that made him very nervous indeed.

He could feel it, whatever it was, flitting at the edges of his conscious mind, and as he watched red suits and dresses mingle with the crowd, he thought he could detect a hint of forced laughter and strained ribaldry amidst the cacophony wherever they passed. Men and women were singled out and encircled, plucked from their cliques like stags separated from the herd. There was no rhyme or reason to those who were chosen; or at least none that he could discern.

Feeling the urge to investigate further, he traced the sacred shape of the Voorish Sign in the air with a finger and let his inner eye flicker open.

The spirit-eye, Carnacki had called it, though St. Cyprian's acquaintances in the Society for Psychical Research insisted that it was merely a very focused form of extrasensory perception. Whatever it was, it had taken him several years to learn how to utilize it safely.

The inability of the human mind to correlate all of its perceptions was one of humanity's built-in defences against the many, *many* predatory malignancies that swam through the outer void. But sometimes you were forced to shuck those evolutionary blinders first thing, lest the sharks snap you up all unawares.

The world became soft at the edges and yet more vibrant as his senses expanded to fill the void left by his thoughts and physical sight. Humans were, by and large, as sensitive to the paranormal as animals were to earthquakes. But they put on blinders instinctively, blocking out everything but what was ahead of them.

He could see the lights of each person's *Ka* flickering like candles in the fog all about him. The Ka, or Odic Force, as Baron Von Reichenbach referred to it, was a force which permeated all living things, to greater or lesser degrees. It wasn't quite a soul or the life-force, but something in-between and indefinable. Some were brighter than others, and some guttered like matches in a breeze.

As he looked about the room, the common factor among those chosen by the red-clad society members became evident. The Ka of each and every one blazed like a torch. He was so taken aback that he didn't realize that he was no longer alone until a hand suddenly fastened on his arm. "What's this, then? A party-crasher?" a woman's voice asked.

His third eye slammed shut, hard enough to send a wave of pain rippling through his mind as he was abruptly wrenched back to reality. St. Cyprian turned, and fought the urge to flinch back from the speaker.

It wasn't that she was ugly, particularly, but that there was an ineffable wrongness about her. Even as he pulled his arm free of her grip, he realized that she was the woman he and Gallowglass had followed inside. She wore a short red dress, red stockings and red gloves. In the dim light, she looked somehow out of proportion, as if her head were too small and her body too big. Her eyes shone with a peculiar, almost lurid light, and he stepped back warily. "I thought it was an open party," he said.

"And you just invited yourself in, is that it?" she said. She smiled in an unnerving manner and patted his hand. "Well, no matter. One more or less is as the gods will." She looked at him in an unpleasant way for a moment, and then handed him a red stamped square of card. "An invitation, if you wish. There are more pleasant entertainments around than this smelly little booze-up." She leaned close, her eyes shining strangely. "I can see that you're a man with a great need in you. A thirst that no amount of gin and fizzes can slake." Her voice slid across his nerves like a bow across a violin's strings and he felt a peculiar muzzy-headedness settle over him, just for a moment. He shook it off, his stomach roiling as he realized what had almost happened. The Strix Society was far more dangerous than he'd thought. "No. Don't speak," she said as she held up a hand. "We'll be leaving in a few minutes, if you'd care to tag along."

"Oh? And where would we be going?"

"Oh not far, darling. Just a few moments, as the bird flies." She tittered, as if at a private joke, and patted his hand again. St. Cyprian's skin crawled at her touch, but he was careful not to let it show on his face. As she moved off through the crowd, he flicked the card up and examined it. It was cheaply done, and the only thing on it was what looked to be a stylized owl's head. Which, given their name, wasn't inappropriate. The Strix of Boios, Plautus and Seneca the Younger was nothing more than the common owl; a bird which had long been regarded as a harbinger of ill-omen in the Mediterranean, divine associations aside.

He tried to spot Gallowglass. He caught sight of her near the bar, and caught her attention. As she looked at him, he raised the card in a silent signal, and she nodded. While they had only known one another for little more than a year, they had already established a somewhat comfortable routine in matters such as this. He would go, and she would follow, ready to render assistance, if necessary.

The crowd was beginning to thin. The woman in red caught the crook of his arm and smiled unctuously up at him. "Come on darling, don't dawdle," she purred. St. Cyprian allowed her to lead him out through a side door, where they joined perhaps a dozen others on what he found to be Coventry Street. Of the dozen, less than half were dressed all in red, though two or three—Mosley among them—wore some item of it on their person. One of the red-clad men clapped Mosley on the shoulder and pumped his hand in an attitude of congratulation.

It *was* an initiation, then. A test, perhaps, of some innate sensitivity. In his brief time at his post, St. Cyprian had encountered more than one society dedicated to collecting individuals with certain abilities and skills, willing or otherwise. He glanced at the woman who still held his arm, and she lavished him with a penetrative stare that he could only describe as possessive. He smiled genially at her, and gave her his best impression of a blithering ass.

He heard a dolorous sound from somewhere above, and looked up to see a swirl of loose feathers and a dark shape winging away. The woman tugged on his arm. "This way," she said. With that, the whole crowd of them began moving along Coventry Street, in the direction of Seven Dials.

It made a depressing sort of sense that the Strix Society had its lair in the midst of such a stew. Barely more than two decades prior, Seven Dials had been more popularly known as St. Giles Rookery, and had been one of the worst slums that London had to offer. The area had become a byword for squalor and depravity, and had hosted more than its fair share of occult-types; palm readers, clairvoyants, herbalists and the like had occupied, and indeed, likely still did occupy, the crooked lanes and hidden storefronts of the area. There were also Bolsheviks, Anarchists and Mafioso crowding each other in the garrets, taverns and side-streets. Too, more than one occult society had settled roots into the coiling streets, including Theosophists, Freemasons, Swedenborgians and the infamous and unlamented Esoteric Order of Thoth-Ra.

St. Cyprian still had nightmares about his abortive encounter with the latter; they'd accidentally awakened a particularly pernicious former pharaoh from his centuries-long slumber. The mummy had gone on a short, but vicious rampage before he and Gallowglass had managed to set it, and the house it was in, on fire. They'd never found what was left of it after the fire brigade had done its work. For weeks afterward, St. Cyprian had kept a wary eye on the newspapers for any sign that the creature might have survived its immolation.

The walk didn't take long, and it wasn't made in silence. People chatted happily and a bottle was passed around as they made their way towards an innocuous row of flats. St. Cyprian participated little in the chatter, and kept one eye on the open air above. More than once, he caught a glimpse of something, several somethings, fluttering above them. Birds, he thought, or even bats, though he couldn't be sure.

The group was herded like so many sheep towards a singularly unprepossessing red door. It opened as they approached, and a hunchback with sandy hair and huge ears stepped aside to admit them, his eyes lingering on each person for an uncomfortable period. St. Cyprian began to suspect that whatever else the Strix Society looked for in its members, subtlety wasn't one of them. Then, maybe subtlety would defeat the purpose. He looked about him at the others chosen, and what he saw wasn't amusement or disgust, but interest and, in a few cases, longing.

In the years following the war, people had begun to look for reassurance where they could find it. The poor went to church, but fraudulent mediums and spiritualists were doing boom business amongst the rich, and the membership rosters of occult societies swelled as traumatized souls sought peace in the houses of mystery.

There was music echoing softly from somewhere in the back of the flat. Most of the non-load-bearing walls had been knocked out, creating the illusion of a far larger space. The wallpaper and the carpet both were a dark, disturbing red, and between them and the music, St. Cyprian fancied for a moment that he was standing in a giant's heart. He could smell the acidic tang of insects and the air felt strangely damp.

He went with the flow, and found himself led through the flat and into what had once been a dining room and kitchen, and was now a species of sitting room. Like the rest of the flat, everything was red; the walls were stained the color of blood and a blood red rug covered part of the floor. The other part had been left bare wood, and, seemingly painted on the boards of the floor was a large, extraordinarily realistic image of an owl. Through an open door at the other end of the room, he spotted a narrow, high-walled garden, empty of life save for thick clusters of ivy which draped the walls and the house, stretching from one to the other like a leafy shroud.

A Victor talking machine sat in one corner, expelling music into the thick air. Drinks were doled out and hushed conversations took place here and there. The party was a muted affair, one of those shindigs where you coughed before you spoke, and then decided not to speak at all, and as he sipped a badly-stirred gin, St. Cyprian had the sense that they were waiting for something. Even as he came to this conclusion, an unseen gong sounded and a woman stepped into the room from the garden.

Where she'd come from, St. Cyprian didn't know, for he'd seen no one outside, and there were precious few places to hide. She glided into the room, a vision of loveliness with more curves than a scenic railway, clad in thin red robes that showed off a gratuitous amount of alabaster flesh, and bestowed a glowing smile on the gathered celebrants. As that smile turned in his direction, he felt his hackles quiver and he quickly hid the resulting flinch in a gulp of gin.

"I am Helen Strix, and I bid all of you welcome," she said. She brushed a lock of dark hair out of her soft, round features, and gestured. "Welcome to my home. May you leave a little of the happiness you bring with you." She held out her hands. "You were all invited because in each of you is something greater, waiting to be freed. My brothers and sisters all possess it as well, and those whom I left behind in Paris, Vienna, Venice and Istanbul. And those who have already freed themselves will help you, tonight, if you wish."

No one spoke. Recalling the muzzy-headedness he had felt earlier, he wondered if he was the only one even truly aware of what was going on. Strix went on. "You shall have your first taste of freedom tonight, in but a few moments. But until then, please...drink and make merry. Fill this lonely house with joy," she said, motioning for the Victor to be wound back up. Her eyes flickered over the crowd and before he could look away, her eyes met his. Her eyes were like swirling pools of molten brass, and he felt something leave him as she gazed at him. His muscles felt like cotton, and his head swam. She swept towards him, a half-smile on her face. "Good evening," she murmured.

"Funny name that," St. Cyprian said. "Strix. Not your average handle, I must say."

"Is it? I hadn't noticed, Mr...?"

St. Cyprian smiled. " St. Cyprian. Charles St. Cyprian. Perhaps you've heard of me?"

"Not in the slightest."

"Oh. Well, you have been out of the country, I suppose," St. Cyprian said. He smiled. "That is right, isn't it? You are newly arrived to our fair Albion, aren't you? Do I detect the faintest hint of a Greek accent?"

She smiled in return and tapped her lips with a finger. "I have been away for some time, I am from all over, and now I am here."

"And why did you come back?"

"Why does anyone?" she said, as she circled him slowly. "You came here looking for something. I can tell." He tensed for a moment, but relaxed as she went on. "What is it that you are missing, Mr. St. Cyprian; Charles, may I call you Charles? Is it a woman, perhaps?" she asked teasingly. "Or a man, maybe? Whatever it is, I can help you find it, if you wish." She stroked his cheek.

"And how would you do that?" he asked. There was a strong smell on the air, like a hawk's roost at midday. His vision blurred for a moment as she leaned close, her breath tickling his ear, and he felt a crackle of power as she did so. Whatever Helen Strix was, she was far from human. And the fear he'd felt earlier was back, stronger than before, and at that moment, he wished he'd gone to the Savoy after all.

"I can show you," she whispered. Then she was whirling away, her robes flaring about her as she clapped her hands. "Bring out the flowers, sisters!"

As she spoke, a number of women, now clad in robes similar to Strix's rather than the red dresses they had been wearing before, entered the room bearing wooden trays. Upon each tray lay small heaps of white flowers. Every person in the room was given a flower. St. Cyprian took his gingerly. The petals were fleshy and curled tight to the thin, pale stem. Faint veins of red ran through them, and he was suddenly struck by a memory of a dead horse, caught on the barbed wire at the Somme and the white folds of decomposing fat which flopped appallingly from its eviscerated body.

"Lower the lights please, Evelyn," Strix said, to one of the women. She looked about, smiling in a pleased, almost matriarchal fashion. "The flowers you hold are from the Balkans. And they are the key to unlocking your inner potential. Eating of their petals is the first step on your road to finding what you seek, be it wealth, love or power. It can all be yours. Eat, and be shown the way." The red-clad members of the Society began to sit or lay down on the floor, eating their flowers as they made themselves comfortable. After a moment, several of the guests followed suit. Others, like St. Cyprian, still stood, uncertain.

Strix smiled at these, and continued, "The second step is concentration. Hold in your mind the vision of one who stands in your way or is the object of your desire." She inclined her head. "We all have them, friends; the woman or man who refuses your love, the banker who ignores your request, the politician, the neighbour, the rival on the pitch, or even the family of a loved one," she said, and gestured towards Mosley, whose face darkened momentarily. "At the root of all the world's ills is man, and as for the world, so for you. Enemies, friends, rivals, obstacles all in your path. Let your mind and spirit slip the tethers of flesh until you fly through the dark like the stirges of legend."

As she spoke, her eyes seemed to reflect the dim light like an animal's. "Find them, find the scent of their soul and fly to their side. Drink of their vitality, fill the emptiness in you and be rewarded with a fulfilment that no material experience can provide." She held up a hand as one of the invitees began to speak. "Do not fret; they shall not be harmed by the experience. And they shall have no knowledge of your visit. But they shall become amenable to you. In time, they may even be considered for membership in our august club, even as you yourselves are."

She held up her hands. "You have until dawn, my friends, for we may only fly by night, when the world is dark and quiet. Fly quickly, and fly sure, and in the morning, you will see that everything is as I promised. Eat and dream and fly my brothers and sisters, and all you desire shall be yours." Her voice reverberated oddly and St. Cyprian was tempted, despite himself. He looked about, and saw slack faces and dull eyes that no amount of booze could explain.

There was a power to her words and gestures that was almost hypnotic, and he knew, in that instant, that Helen Strix needed no flower to feed on the vitality of others. She did it with her eyes and voice, and if he allowed himself to be lulled, he would be as lost as those he'd come with.

Hastily, he put the flower in his pocket and made for the garden. No one tried to stop him. He closed the door behind him as he walked into the garden. Outside, the cool night air helped clear his head, and the muzzy feeling evaporated. He could think clearly again, and with that clarity came a cold surge of fear. The situation was far worse than he'd first thought, and required immediate action. He was considering just what that action might be when someone said, "What are you doing out here?"

He turned. Oswald Mosley glared at him from the stoop. "I say, did you hear me? What are you doing?" he asked again, as he closed the door behind him.

"Just getting a bit of fresh air, what? Bit close in there for my constitution, you know?" St. Cyprian replied, smiling doltishly. "Ruddy strange party, if you want my opinion."

"I'm sure I don't. Come back inside, there's a good chap." Mosley reached for him, and St. Cyprian let the other man grab his sleeve. As he lurched towards Mosley, he widened his eyes comically.

"I say, is that you Mosley?"

Mosley's eyes narrowed. "You know me?"

"Do I?"

"You just said you did," Mosley growled. "Who are you?"

"Who wants to know?" St. Cyprian said.

"I asked you first," Mosley snapped. He made to grab St. Cyprian, and the latter staggered back, out of reach and away from the door. Mosley followed him. As they reached the middle of the garden, St. Cyprian straightened.

"My name is St. Cyprian. Your father-in-law to be sent me," he said softly. Mosley stopped. His dark eyes widened slightly and he frowned.

"What? Why?" he demanded.

"I think you know why, Mosley."

Mosley smirked. "It's none of his business, I should think. And yours neither, whoever the devil you are."

"Oh you'd be wrong there. This is indeed my business, if what I suspect

"What are you doing out here?"

about what's going on in there is true. Is that how they got you? A promise, then a taste and then...what?" St. Cyprian cocked his head. "Curzon was looking quite ill. What would you know about that, I wonder?"

Mosley's face flushed. "I wouldn't know anything about that."

"I think you do. And I think you had best come with me, for the sake of your soul, if not his," St. Cyprian said harshly.

"I'm not leaving," Mosley growled. "And neither are you." He swung a fist. St. Cyprian easily avoided the blow, and caught the other man in the belly with a swift blow of his own. Mosley wheezed and bent forward. St. Cyprian caught him easily and dragged him backwards, away from the door, towards the back wall. Once they were far enough away, he caught Mosley a blow on the jaw. Mosley's eye lids fluttered and he dropped.

"Hsst." He looked up, and saw a familiar face peering at him from the top of the wall. "You didn't half knock the bugger silly, did you?" Gallowglass said wonderingly.

"What in God's name are you doing up there?" he hissed.

"Empty flat back here, innit? Came through the door, didn't I? Is that him?" Gallowglass whispered back, beaming down at him like the Cheshire cat.

"Who else would it be?" he spat. "Here...help me get him over the wall."

They manhandled Mosley over the garden wall with much muffled cursing on Gallowglass' part and furtive glances at the door on St. Cyprian's. As Mosley's shoes vanished over the top, St. Cyprian grabbed the ivy and heaved himself up, scrambling over with as much dignity as he could muster. Even as he dropped down, he heard the door open, and a voice call out. He shot a warning look at Gallowglass, who mimed slitting her throat. He shook his head urgently. After a moment, they heard the door shut, and St. Cyprian hefted Mosley over his shoulders. He'd carried enough wounded men in the trenches that Mosley's weight was little bother to him. "Let's go," he said.

Gallowglass led him through the abandoned house and out onto the opposite street where the Crossley sat waiting. He deposited Mosley in the back, and then climbed behind the wheel. They were silent as they made their way back towards Kensington. Mosley barely stirred, and Gallowglass watched him, a cosh in one hand. Only when they had drawn within sight of No. 427 again, did she say, "Sure this is smart?"

"Smarter than playing out that particular string any longer. Curzon was right, the Strix Society are a bad lot. Mosley might be a perisher, but there's worse things to be." St. Cyprian parked the Crossley and between them, they managed to get Mosley into the house without too much trouble. He dropped him into one of the chairs before the fireplace and sent Gallowglass to fetch a suitable set of restraints. "Get the Glastonbury chains. I have a feeling they'll be more efficacious than the metal variety. Oh, and a mortar and pestle, and put on some tea."

"Tea?"

"I would murder for a cuppa. Pick up your heels, assistant mine. The night wears on, and time is not on our side," St. Cyprian said. Gallowglass hastened to obey.

Kidnapping Mosley had been a spur of the moment decision. He wouldn't know whether it had been a bad one until it was over and done with, however. He took the white flower out of his pocket and examined it briefly before stuffing it back out of sight. If he was right, they only had an hour at most before Mosley's comrades tracked them down, in one form or another.

It took a certain degree of concentration to project the immaterial self from the physical, but he had no doubt that at least a few members of the members of the Society had the experience necessary. And they had Mosley's spiritual scent, if not his own, to lead them to their quarry. He looked down at the former. Mosley was stirring. St. Cyprian considered punching him again. Mosley had the sort of features that begged for a beating. Gallowglass returned before he had to make the decision, carrying the Glastonbury chains.

Despite the name, they weren't actually chains as such, but rather strips of bark and branches, woven together to make an improvised rope of sorts. The bark and branches had been harvested from the hawthorn trees of Glastonbury, where it was said to have been planted by Joseph of Arimathea. Hawthorn was proof against most malignant sorceries and psychical afflictions, and he'd used the Glastonbury chains to good effect more than once.

Working quickly, he and Gallowglass tied the hawthorn about Mosley. Mosley moaned. He tried to rise, his eyelids fluttering, but the hawthorn prevented him. "Think it'll hold him?" Gallowglass said.

"It worked on that possessed chappie in Durham last April," St. Cyprian said as he retrieved a lacquered box of oriental design from the bookshelf and flipped it open. Inside were a number of paper satchels full of dried flowers. Before he could extract one, he heard a thin whine from the direction of the window. Something that might have been a bird's shadow passed across it. Across the street, the lights on the Embankment went out, one by one, casting the street and the river both into darkness.

"Feel that," Gallowglass said.

St. Cyprian nodded slowly. There was a pall in the air, and a sour taste on his tongue. He felt as he had on the walk to Seven Dials. Something was watching them, spying on them from the windows and peeping through the keyholes. The glass frosted slightly, as if something were breathing on it. "We have company."

Gallowglass' hand dipped for the pistol holstered beneath her arm. St. Cyprian caught her hand. "No," he said. "They are things of spirit. They must be fought the same way." He gave the box a shake. "*Arbutus Unede*, to use the scientific classification. The Romans used its smoke to chase away evil and cleanse dwelling places of noisome spirits," he said as he tossed a sachet into the fireplace. A thin, pale smoke boiled out, and Mosley's thrashing stilled. The pall in the room seemed as if it were about to disperse, but then it redoubled. There was a sound like roaches skittering in the corners, and the lights flickered.

"Quickly, mash some of the arbutus up," he said, gesturing to the pestle and bowl. "We'll need some to go in the tea. And some powdered emerald as well."

"Emerald?" Gallowglass asked.

"I knew you hadn't read the Hermes Trismegitus," he said, shooting her a glare.

"I was getting 'round to it," Gallowglass said.

"Getting 'round to it, she says. Emerald draws out spiritual poisons, as well as physical ones. Oh, and some crushed fern frond as well. We'll need that to expel whatever is in him now. It's vital that we cleanse him of those foul flowers."

The windows began to rattle in their frames, as if something quick and heavy were thrashing against them. The door shuddered and the lights flickered again. Then, all at once, everything went quiet. Gallowglass paused, pestle in hand. "Think they're gone?"

"No." St. Cyprian stepped quickly to the bookshelf and snatched down a strangely etched clay pot. He wrenched the top off and scooped out a handful of the dust within. He flung the dust out in a wide circle and the air took on a shimmery haze reminiscent of the open desert at midday. "But let's see what the powder of Ibn Ghazi has to show us."

Ghostly shapes darted through the settling dust. He had no idea how they'd gotten in; the flat was protected against all but the most powerful of spirits, and these should have remained safely outside, rattling the windows. But they were inside now, and intent on mischief.

They were at once avian, insectile and humanoid, and they made no sound as they sprang for St. Cyprian. He felt something clammy seize him and cried out. They were things of spirit, rather than flesh, but they were as hungry as any earthly predator. As they clutched at him, thin, familiar voices brushed at his ears like the wings of moths and he felt pinpricks of pain up and down his arms and neck. He fell back, slamming into the bookcase. *Now look who's inviting themselves in,* something whispered shrilly in his ear. He recognized the voice of the woman in the red dress, and others as well. The whole crew of them were out in force, and he felt them tearing at his Ka with ghostly fangs.

"Oi," Gallowglass barked, "Catch!"

St. Cyprian felt something smack his chest and he caught it automatically. It was a sachet of arbutus. Clutching it in both hands, he stumbled towards the fireplace and flung it in. Smoke erupted from the fireplace, sweeping over him. He coughed and sank down to one knee. He could feel the hold of the vampire-spirits weakening. They were carried away by the smoke as if it were a strong gale and they were nothing more than leaves. His ears echoed with tinny shrieks and faint wails as the smoke drove their foes from No. 427 and back out into the night.

Wheezing, his stomach churning, he nodded weakly to Gallowglass as she passed him more arbutus. He fed it into the fire, wondering how long it would take him to replace his stock. The front door banged on its hinges, blown open. He could hear the trees on the Embankment rustling as if in a strong wind, and amidst the creak and hiss, he thought he could hear a woman's voice; the voice of Helen Strix. He heard the screech of an owl, and the snap of wings and then, laughter.

Mosley began to thrash again, and he made a sound like a dying dog. He bayed and squirmed, but the hawthorn held him in his chair. St. Cyprian, clutching a handful of arbutus, staggered to the door, and stared out at the Embankment. A thin sliver of daylight was creeping across the city, and the night was retreating.

Helen Strix watched him, her face as still and stiff as that of a statue. She still wore her robes, and they flapped and flared in the wind. Her eyes sought his, and then slid past him. He heard a moan, and then a thump and spun about to see that Mosley's chair had toppled over. Gallowglass rubbed her fist. She joined him at the door. "Silly bugger tried to get up, didn't he?"

St. Cyprian heard a sound like a bird of prey sighting its next meal, and he turned back in time to see Strix raise a hand. Her shape wavered like a wisp of smoke. She stretched and spread, growing larger and larger as the dark gave way to the light, and then, like a soap bubble grown to its limit, she vanished.

"What is she?" Gallowglass breathed. If he hadn't known better, he'd have sworn she was frightened.

"I don't know." He stepped back and closed the door. "Get the tea ready." As Gallowglass prepared the tea, he hauled Mosley upright. Working quickly, he mixed the concoction and, with Gallowglass' help, poured it down the unconscious man's throat. He massaged Mosley's throat until he was sure he'd swallowed the tea, and then he waved Gallowglass back. "Wake up," he snapped. He slapped Mosley's cheek lightly. The man groaned and stirred. "Wake up, Oswald."

"What...I...you!" Mosley hissed. He jerked forward, and then slumped back. "I can't...I can't feel her anymore," he said. He sounded bereft, like a child who'd lost his mother. "Why can't I feel her?"

"You're welcome," St. Cyprian said. He snipped the hawthorn strands, and Mosley's face took on a particular hue as he suddenly toppled out of the chair and emptied the contents of his stomach onto the rug. "Oh really now, must you?" St. Cyprian said as he stepped back. What came out of Mosley's stomach was tarry and reeking, and undigested bits of white squirmed in its midst like maggots. St. Cyprian took another step back. "Well, yes, in that case, I suppose you rather must, what?"

Mosley shuddered and heaved for several minutes. St. Cyprian wondered how long he'd been under Helen Strix's spell, and tried not to think about what might have come out of him if Curzon had waited a few more days before coming to see him. When he'd finished, Mosley collapsed on the rug and rolled to the side, panting like a dog.

"What is that stuff?" Gallowglass said, her face wrinkled in disgust.

"Something I'd recommended you not touch with your bare hands when you clean it up," St. Cyprian said as he dropped to his haunches beside Mosley.

"Me?"

"Yes, and do be quick about it. I rather fear that it's eating through the rug." He patted Mosley on the shoulder. "There, there, old thing. Better out than in, as my mother used to say."

Mosley glared blearily up at him. "What did you do to me?"

"Nothing much. Just kept your soul from the doorstep of eternal damnation," St. Cyprian said. "Hardly anything at all, really."

"What...?"

St. Cyprian stood. "You were playing a dangerous game, Mr. Mosley. One you were fated to lose. I merely bought out your stake, as it were. I should stick to politics, if I were you. Less chance of you making a spectacular ass of yourself."

Mosley closed his eyes and his head thumped the floor in a defeated fashion. Gallowglass looked down at him. "Is he normal again?"

"As normal as he ever was," St. Cyprian said. "We've driven out the things he invited in. We'll burn the rug, just to be sure." He looked at her. "It was the flowers, you see. I recognized them right off, though there's not a proper name for them. I first saw them when I was with Carnacki in Greece. They grow on the graves of vampires, or so the local folklore has it. There's a book on the shelves, one of my predecessors' journals, somewhere that has a few of them pressed between the pages. Plucked from the lonely mountain grave of Sir Francis Varney himself." He pulled the crushed and crumpled flower he'd been given in Seven Dials from his pocket and showed it to her. "If eaten once or twice, the blasted things bring out the worst in a chap, especially if he's of a psychical persuasion like Oswald there. They don't become vampires, but something quite close, I fear. If eaten more than that...well. Who can say?"

"Helen Strix," Gallowglass replied.

St. Cyprian looked at Mosley, moaning on the carpet, and nodded. "I'm afraid so. Whatever she is, she needs to be dealt with. And as soon as possible." He took a deep breath and nodded. "Right. I'll see to her. You keep an eye on him. There's only one way to be sure that he doesn't relapse, and that's to cut off his supply." He went to fireplace and pulled down the xiphos, in its sheath. He looped the cord over his head, and the sword dangled comfortably against his hip. After testing it to make sure that it wouldn't be too awkward, he unsheathed the blade and laid it atop the mantle. Then, working quickly, he hefted the pestle bowl and smeared the juices of the mashed arbutus along the blade.

When he was satisfied, he sheathed the xiphos and took the small chest down off the mantle. He set it down on the floor and ran his hand over it. The chest was old and ornate, with brass clasps and hinges. Ancient scorch marks marred the treated wood. The Gothic characters inscribed on the lock harkened back to its original owner, Prince Rupert of the Rhine. He opened it carefully, as if something within might leap out to strike him. Which, given what was in the chest, wouldn't be unexpected.

"From ghoulies and ghosties and long-leggedy beasties and things that go bump in the night, good lord, deliver us," he murmured softly as he examined what lay inside. There were oddly colored stones of many types, the fangs of beasts as yet unidentified by science and tangled knots of amulets of varying ages and degrees of effectiveness. And beneath them all was the odd shape of the Monas Glyph.

Created by Dr. John Dee in the rein of Elizabeth the First, the esoteric sigil was a composite of various astrological and religious symbols, combining ankh, cruciform and crescent. It was a potent artefact, but one he only rarely employed, and only when faced with something worse than the run of the mill nightmares. He had seen Carnacki use it to exorcise visitors from the Outer Spheres more than once, and Dee was said to have employed it in putting paid to the last English dragon.

He extracted the Glyph and held it up. The weak streamers of sunlight that came through the window ran across the swoops and curves of it in odd ways. He blinked and looked away. In its own way, it was almost as disturbing as what he intended to employ it against. It sapped the vitality of its user and put the senses on a knife edge for days afterward.

He pulled on his greatcoat and stuffed the Glyph in a pocket. Outside, a new day was dawning. Weak sunlight drifted through the windows and crawled across the floor. Mosley shuddered and rolled away from it. Gallowglass looked at St. Cyprian. "Are you sure you want to go alone?"

"Someone has to watch our guest. And it is my lot, what? Responsibilities of the office and all that." He took her hand and patted it. "Never you fear, Miss Gallowglass. I shall be back directly."

"Leave off," she muttered, jerking her hand out of his. He smiled and left her standing there. Outside, the day was crisp and cool, and sad, gray clouds rolled across the sky. He hoped the inevitable rain would hold off long enough for him to do what needed to be done, but he couldn't count on it. He would have to be quick.

The drive to Seven Dials took less time than he would've liked, and more than he hoped. The red door hadn't vanished, as he'd half-suspected it might. No, Helen Strix was waiting for him, that much he was certain of. He sat in the Crossley and eyed the door, considering. Then, with a sigh, he got out and went to the door. It wasn't locked. It opened with barely a whisper. No one seemed to be at home.

He stepped inside. The floor creaked beneath the carpet, and he heard something scurrying about somewhere above him. A draft caused the door to thump shut, startling him. He felt as if he were walking into a lion's den. He made his way to the back room. It was empty. Wherever the Strix Society was now, they weren't here. Perhaps they'd fled with the dawn, counting on their president and high priestess to deal with him.

As if that thought had been a signal, laughter suddenly echoed from everywhere and nowhere, springing from wall to wall and floor to ceiling, growing in volume until it threatened to deafen him. St. Cyprian clapped his hands to his ears. The room seemed to tilt and heave and his eyes strayed to the floor.

The owl painted on the floorboards was gone. Instead, Helen Strix's face leered up at him. Her smile was wickedness itself, and her eyes, two dimensional as they were, gazed up at him with a malignant gleam, as if she could see into the darkest, nastiest corners of his soul. Her eyes grew brighter and brighter, and he felt her talons pry at his mind. He'd been a fool to come alone; he'd been a fool to challenge her at all. He couldn't tell whether those were his thoughts or hers.

He felt a wash of heat, and though there was no fire, he felt flames lick his flesh. He heard screams, and the roar of crumbling brick. Strange shadows danced on the walls, and his ears throbbed with the grinding hum of aircraft engines. He heard the clash of swords and the bark of rifles, as a city, London perhaps, or something older and far away, fell to invaders. And then, a woman's voice, "Blood ran in torrents, drenched was all of the earth. As apt now as it was then, and will be, don't you think?"

St. Cyprian opened his eyes. Helen Strix stood before him, an amused smile on her face. "I wondered if you'd come," she said. "It's rare you find such a delightful blend of courage and utter stupidity in these sad, gray times."

"Who are you?" he croaked.

She ignored the question. Her robes rustled softly as she circled him. He was reminded of a panther he'd seen in the zoo, all smooth rolling muscle and predatory grace. "I smell magics on you. I thought I caught a whiff of sorcery last night, when we met. A little magus, come to pit his goetia against *la belle dame sans merci*, eh?" She smiled and held out a hand. "Oh what can ail thee, knight-at-arms, alone and palely loitering?"

St. Cyprian cleared his throat. "Keats," he said. "I met a lady in the meads, full beautiful, a faery's child, her hair was long, her foot was light, and her eyes were wild."

She clapped her hands in delight. "Very good! Of course, my father was no mere faery, but something else entirely," she said, "A being of divine hungers and deeds." She smiled. "Both of which I have matched him in, measure for measure down the long red road of years, when I could. Men have gone to war for me, and they will again."

"Yes, well, I'm sure he's proud. However, I'm afraid I must insist that you desist and decamp, post-haste," St. Cyprian said, following her with his eyes. "Maybe go back to Paris. Or Berlin, perhaps? I'm sure a woman of your...inclinations would enjoy herself there." He took his cigarette case out of his coat and popped it open, fighting to keep his hands from trembling.

"Oh, but I only just got back," Helen said.

"Yes, and you've made quite the impression on the scene, I daresay, but I really must insist," he said, as she continued to circle him. He was reminded of the way a falcon drew closer and closer to its prey just before it struck.

"Why? What have I done to offend you so, little magus?"

"Me? Nothing. The Foreign Minister, on the other hand..."

She laughed. "Ah. So you are an Odysseus, then, fighting Agamemnon's war."

"Oh, are we back to that?" he said, feigning boredom. "I went to Eton, my good woman. I know Homer and Virgil better than my own family."

"I knew them as well," she said. "Who do you think told them of those long ago warriors and their far away fates? I betrayed the Trojans and the Greeks both. The former I led in Bacchic rites, so that they were in no position to defend themselves when the Greeks came with sword and fire. And the latter I did torment with the voices of their loved ones left behind as they crouched in the stinking belly of their wooden offering." She licked her lips. "I hated them all, you see. All the petty men who shuddered at me."

"I'm sure the feeling was mutual," he said. "I know you now, Helen Strix. You are that which cries by night, without food or drink, with head below and tips of feet above, a harbinger of war and civil strife for men," he recited, as his hand dipped for the hilt of the xiphos. One quick thrust and he could have it in her heart.

Helen laughed again. "Oh it has been ages since I heard that. Boios, isn't it? Well, you did say you went to Eton." And then, in the blink of an eye, she was on him. She was faster than he expected, and she had filched the sword and its sheath from inside his coat and flung them aside before he even realized that she was moving. Her fingers were at his throat a moment later and he gurgled as he felt her fingers snap shut like the talons of a hawk. "You came during the day. That means you have some idea of what I am. It's the wrong idea, of course, but you're not the first to make that mistake. Aeneas and Megapenthes did as well." She smiled widely. "I am no *empusa* or *vrykolakas*, to be sent wafting away with an iron nail in my heart." He hammered at her forearm with his fists. It was like pounding on stone. "I am *ennoia*, and eternal."

"You remind me of Aeneas," she continued, lifting him off of his feet. "Around the jaw, mostly. There's Trojan blood in you, I'd warrant. Then, there's a bit of Brutus in every Briton, according to that old fraud, Monmouth." She smiled. "Did you know that they came here originally to exile me? To bury my lead coffin on this soggy little island? Then, they decided to stay." Her smiled faded. "They buried me anyway. And built their city over me. I felt it grow. It fed on me, and there is something of me in every street and cul-de-sac in Londinium. This city fed off of me, until a great fire freed me and I escaped on the wind of ash and smoke. And now that I have returned, I will feed off of it."

"That...doesn't explain anything, actually," St. Cyprian croaked as he tried to pry her fingers from his throat. Her arm, so frail looking, was like a bar of iron, and her fingers like the jaws of a trap.

"It doesn't, doesn't it?" She pulled him close. Her smile was back, and sharp enough to make him bleed. "I could explain so many things to you, if you but let me. I would happily let you join my society for the price of a kiss...a single kiss, Mr. St. Cyprian. Is that so heavy a price to bear?"

"I truly, from the law of that Majesty, command thee to go away now most calmly to your place, without murmur and commotion, and without harm to us and the circle of other men. In the name of the Father, the Son and the Holy Ghost, Amen," St. Cyprian rasped, slashing the air before her eyes with two fingers in a curious motion. It was a long shot, but it was better than nothing.

Helen's laugh was like the peal of a bell. She shook him slightly, and her thumbnail traced the hollow of his throat. "I am older than your desert god, little sorcerer. And I shall cause a commotion if I wish."

"That makes two of us," Gallowglass said. Exactly where she had come from, St. Cyprian couldn't say, but he felt a thrill of relief as the barrel of her Webley-Fosbery tapped the back of Helen's head. Before the smaller woman could pull the trigger, however, Helen whirled with inhuman speed, swinging St. Cyprian around like a sackcloth. Gallowglass ducked and fired. Helen shrieked as the bullet grazed her cheek. She staggered back, clutching at her face.

"Where?" he croaked.

"Followed you, didn't I? Can't let you out alone, can I?" Gallowglass said,

"I am ennoia, and eternal."

braced and ready for whatever Helen decided to do next. She glanced at him. "You paid for the cab, by the way." Shaking his head, St. Cyprian fumbled in his coat pocket for the Monas Glyph. He hadn't come unprepared, but Helen was quicker than he'd anticipated. Then, if she was who she claimed to be, she'd had more time than most to learn how to fight.

Helen's screams rose to an ear-splitting pitch and then broke off into a flurry of cursing. She lowered her hands. St. Cyprian saw that Gallowglass' bullet had torn open her cheek, and something like tar dripped down the line of her jaw. "My *face*," she hissed. The sound was guttural, and savage.

"Try launching a thousand ships now," Gallowglass chortled nastily. She extended her pistol. Helen went for her, moving like a leopardess. She sprang forward, her hands extended like claws. Gallowglass fired. The revolver bucked in her hand as the cylinder emptied. Helen twisted in mid-lunge, moving with boneless grace. Bullets skidded across her bare flesh, leaving black marks. To St. Cyprian, they looked like cracks in marble.

His fingers found the hard, metal disk of bronze they'd been searching for even as Helen crashed into Gallowglass, catapulting them backwards, across the room and out of through the back door in an explosion of wood. St. Cyprian snatched his fallen sword up and tore it from its sheath as he raced after the two women. He had no idea what Helen was, exactly, but he hoped the sword could stop her.

As he reached the door, he saw that they had broken apart, and now faced each other in the garden. Gallowglass had dropped her pistol in the tussle and Helen's pale fingers were crooked like claws and her lips peeled back from long, even teeth.

"I saw the towers of Ilium burned, you little wretch, and the crude hovels of this pestilential pile as well," Helen snarled as she advanced on Gallowglass, sidling around the thin shafts of sunlight which pierced the ivy overhead. "And I'll see it burn again, before I'm done."

She lunged, the shredded remnants of her robes spreading around her like wings. Gallowglass' hand dipped into her coat and reappeared with a balisong, which she expertly flicked open. The silvery blade danced across Helen's hand as she clawed for Gallowglass. Her other hand caught the smaller woman a blow that sent her flying backwards into the ivy along the back wall.

Sword in one hand, St. Cyprian scooped up a chunk of the broken door frame in the other even as Helen turned. She hissed and he smashed the hunk of wood across her face. It exploded into fragments, and she staggered. St. Cyprian thrust the sword towards her, but her hands snapped up, catching the blade between her palms.

He didn't hesitate, but instead threw all of his weight against the pommel of the sword. Helen barely budged. "No, I think not," she hissed. She made to wrench it out of his hands, but her eyes widened suddenly and she released the blade with a wail. Smoke rose from her hands and she staggered. More crack-like lines spread up her arms.

"The juice of the arbutus leaf," St. Cyprian said. "Burnt, it drives away unclean spirits, as your followers found out last night. Mashed, it does much the same." He advanced on her, and she backed away, eyes blazing and teeth bared. "I don't know what you are, exactly, but I can hurt you even so." He stretched his sword up and slashed at the ivy overhead, allowing in the sunlight.

"I'll pluck out your heart and eat it," she snarled, cringing back from the light that spilled down into the dark garden.

"Charming," he said, hoping she couldn't hear the tremor in his voice. He reached into his coat pocket and pulled out the Monas Glyph. "In the name of Thanatos, I command thee; in the name of Cthonios, I bind thee; in the name of Hades, I blind thee," he intoned, stepping forward. The Glyph began to grow warm in his hand. The sunlight reflected off of its strangely swirling surface. Helen cast up a hand, as if to block out the sight of it.

"Death has no claim on me, nor the gloomy god," she snarled.

"No? Seems like it's doing the trick to me," he said, pursuing her. "On your feet, Miss Gallowglass," he called. "No malingering on duty, if you please."

Gallowglass thrust her face through the ivy. Her cap was askew and her jaw was purpling on one side, but her eyes were bright. "Got a punch like a stevedore," she said. She clambered out of the ivy and snatched up her pistol. As she began to reload, St. Cyprian drove Helen back towards the open sunlight with the Glyph.

Helen made a low sound in her throat as she entered the light, and faint curlicues of smoke rose from the black marks on her flesh. She slapped at her skin, like a woman beset by stinging insects, and her face contorted into an animalistic snarl. The Glyph grew hot in his hand, and he knew that somehow, in some way, she was fighting its power. His heart sank. Whatever she was, she was more powerful than he had feared.

"What do we do now?" Gallowglass asked as she snapped her Webley shut.

"Something clever," St. Cyprian said. He cut his eyes upwards. The sun was already vanishing behind the clouds. Gallowglass' bullets would be of no help. And his talisman wasn't doing any obvious good, either. That left the sword.

"That'd be a first," Gallowglass muttered and took aim. Helen hissed as she heard the Webley being cocked. St. Cyprian readied himself. His heart thudded against his ribs. He would only get one chance.

Helen sprang.

St. Cyprian lunged smoothly, with a fencer's grace, and the tip of the xiphos caught her in the breast. Black fluid and smoke burst from her mouth as she fell, pulling the sword from his hands. There was a sound like crockery striking stone, and her white flesh came apart all at once. Something large and feathery sprang upwards, passing through the ivy before he could catch clear sight of it. He heard the snap of wings and then it was gone, leaving only a raw, harsh smell, like spoiled blood, and a few spiralling crimson feathers to mark its passage.

Gallowglass raised her pistol, and then lowered it. She looked at St. Cyprian. "You call that clever?"

"It worked, didn't it?"

She shook her head and sank to her haunches beside what was left of Helen Strix. She used the barrel of her pistol to prod the hard, white pieces that, to St. Cyprian's eyes, looked like the pieces of an egg shell. "What was she?"

"Something old," he said as he retrieved his sword. He looked at Gallowglass. "Thank you, by the way."

She shrugged and stood. "Like I said, somebody has to watch out for you."

"And who's watching out for Mosley?"

"The tinned sprouts," she said as she holstered her pistol. At his quizzical look, she clarified, "I locked him in the pantry. Stuffed some of those arbutus blossoms down his trousers, just in case." She looked up. "Think she's buggered off for good?"

St. Cyprian was silent for a moment, thinking of the fire he'd felt, and what he'd seen. Had she been showing him the past, or the future? He shook his head. "God, I hope so." He heard the faint cry of bird, what kind he couldn't say, and he shivered.

"But somehow, I doubt it."

THE END

SO...WHO IS THE ROYAL OCCULTIST?

Formed during the reign of Elizabeth I, the post of the Royal Occultist, or 'the Queen's Conjurer' as it was known, was created for and first held by the diligent amateur, Dr. John Dee, in recognition for an unrecorded service to the Crown.

The title has passed through a succession of hands since, some good, some bad; the list is a long one, weaving in and out of the margins of British history and including such luminaries as the 1st Earl of Holderness and Thomas Carnacki.

Now, in the wake of the Great War, the title and offices have fallen to Charles St. Cyprian who, accompanied by his apprentice Ebe Gallowglass, defends the British Empire against threats occult, otherworldly, infernal and divine even as the wider world lurches once more on the path to war...

The Royal Occultist is the man—or woman—who stands between the British Empire and its occult enemies, be they foreign, domestic, human, demonic or some form of worm of unusual size. If there are satyrs running amok in Somerset or werewolves in Wolverhampton, the Royal Occultist will be there to see them off.

The current Royal Occultist is Charles St. Cyprian, who's best described as Rudolph Valentino by way of Bertie Wooster. In the same vein, his assistant, Ebe Gallowglass, is Louise Brooks by way of Emma Peel. St. Cyprian is the brains and Gallowglass is the muscle; he likes to talk things out, and she likes to shoot things until they die. Together, they defend the British Empire against a variety of gribbly monsters, secret societies and eldritch occurrences.

St. Cyprian and Gallowglass made their first appearance in 2010 in the short story, "Krampusnacht". They have since appeared in close to thirty short stories, in a variety of anthologies and magazines, all of which are still currently available. Some of them are even available for free!

The first novel to feature the duo, THE WHITECHAPEL DEMON,

was released in 2013 by Emby Press and is available via Amazon.com and Smashwords. The Whitechapel Demon sees St. Cyprian and Gallowglass go up against a secret society of murderists and an other-dimensional doppelgänger of one of history's most notorious killers. The book serves as an introduction to the world of the Royal Occultist as well as delivering an exciting adventure for new readers and old fans alike to enjoy. The next novel in the series, THE JADE SUIT OF DEATH, will be available sometime in 2014.

To visit the Royal Occultist site, set your browser for: http://royaloccultist. wordpress.com/

You can also keep track of the latest Royal Occultist news via the series' Facebook page at: https://www.facebook.com/RoyalOccultist

A number of the Royal Occultist stories are available in audio format via Bandcamp at: https://royaloccultist.bandcamp.com/

JOSH REYNOLDS - is a freelance writer of moderate skill and exceptional confidence. He has written a bit, and some of it was even published. His work has appeared in anthologies such as Miskatonic River Press' Horror for the Holidays, and in periodicals such as Innsmouth Magazine and Lovecraft eZine. In addition to his own work, a full list of which can be found at   http://joshuamreynolds.wordpress.com/ Josh has written for several tie-in franchises, including Gold Eagle's Executioner line as well as Black Library's Warhammer Fantasy line.

And if, after finishing "The Strix Society", you're interested in reading more about Charles St. Cyprian and the Royal Occultist, make sure to check out http://royaloccultist.wordpress.com/ for links to other stories, as well as free fiction and contests!

THE LOST WIFE OF THOMAS TAN

A SGT. JANUS TALE
BY JIM BEARD

Looking out at the falling snow from underneath the Raynham Road Bridge, the nub of a pencil in my barely-sensate fingers, I am scribbling this on bits of crumpled paper found in my pockets. There is a curious pain in my arm and in my chest. My head is swimming. We thought this was finished. The Sergeant thought this was finished. Apparently, that is not the case.

Perhaps this will be the last thing I ever write, which is a shame because I always liked to write. But I will endeavor to begin it and to finish it, and hope that it will find its way into someone's hands who will welcome its record of the events of the past few days.

I first met Roman Janus last May, during the flooding. Of course I knew of him; we all know of him in town, and in the city, too. He is of average height and build, with sandy hair and strange eyes, enormous presence, and calm demeanor. He dresses like a military man, though his uniform exhibits no signs of rank or decoration. There is a scent about him of books, though his hands are those of a worker.

Little thought I gave him before the day when I found myself shoulder-to-shoulder with the man, lifting heavy bags of sand to bolster a wall that threatened to give way from the weight of the water behind it. Throughout that long, arduous day we worked together well, albeit silently, for the most part. We made quite a team, if I do say so myself. Then, having been relieved by incoming hands, Janus and I introduced ourselves to each other and he told me the strangest thing. I will never forget it as long as I shall, well, for whatever time I may have left.

He said, "Miriam has asked me to find you. She cannot find her way."

Why strange? You see, my wife, my dear, sweet, lovely Miriam, has been dead for ten long years.

And I am responsible for her death.

—⫸|⫷—

Mount Airy Eagle
Late Edition, Sunday, May 10th

Flood Waters Threaten Town
"Worst Flooding in Decades," Say Some

After a pronounced rain storm that lasted nearly six days without cessation, the Airy River rose beyond record levels and flooded the entire area of Mount Airy and neighboring villages. Though now subsided, the flooding has caused widespread property damage as well as robbing several townspeople of their lives.

The first day of flooding brought the deluge to homesteads along the riverbank, but by the second day it had reached Mount Airy proper. Mayor Spinnett called for emergency measures to insure public safety and asked that all able-bodied men assemble in the town square to build several bulwarks against the spread of the flood. It is estimated that one-hundred and twenty men answered that call and worked for nearly seventy-two hours to clear the area of citizens and to construct walls and reinforce existing structures.

Many longtime residents of Mount Airy said that they had never seen such flooding before.

The Mount Airy Fire Department was called to the scene of at least two fires that broke out due to electrical wiring exposed to the flood waters. One Fireman, George Masters, expired from injuries he sustained while fighting a blaze at Michaels Bakery on High Street, while three of his fellows were hospitalized due to their injuries at the same location.

Noted "spirit-breaker" Sgt. Roman Janus of Raynham Road was seen attending Fireman Masters alongside two physicians at the scene of the fire, though it is not currently known whether or not the man had expired by that time. Moments after Masters was removed from the site, Sgt. Janus was witnessed aiding workers who were building a temporary dam along Mason Avenue, where he remained for at least twenty-four hours.

One of the worst scenes of destruction brought about by the flood waters was at the cemetery of St. Barnabas Church on the east side of Mount Airy. Graves and mausoleums, some of them dating to one-hundred years old or more, were washed away by the flooding, as well as trees, fencing, and sheds. The priests of St. Barnabas report that more than eighty of the ninety-seven graves encompassed by the cemetery have been disturbed and, they fear, are unrecoverable. The Church is calling for help from the community to search for remains and artifacts.

Mayor Spinnett will speak on this matter and on other efforts to rebuild areas damaged by the flood tomorrow, Monday the 11th, at Town Hall.

—*/|*\—

I have done many things in my life of which I am not proud; it would be pointless to go into them here and now. Perhaps they will all be revealed when I am gone, but suffice to say that I had long answered to a certain individual and had done his dark bidding, which quite often entailed the destruction of his enemies and of their assumed plots against him. In return, I had been rewarded with creature comforts and had seen much of the wide world.

But I had never truly been a happy man—until I met Miriam. Miriam changed everything.

She was not well in her own mind; I see that plainly now, but for the first year of our marriage it was not clear at all and I suffered many a day and night in confusion over it. You see, Miriam was not always herself and she could become easily lost, both in physical space and in spirit. But I loved her, oh Lord how I loved her, and we crafted a semblance of a life together despite her illness and my being a very, very bad man. I kept her hidden away from the prying eyes of the world and, so I thought at the time, from my master.

One day, after a particularly onerous night of Miriam's wanderings, I spoke a word to my master after receiving his orders, the likes of which he was greatly unfamiliar:

"No."

And then I left his presence and wandered myself for a time and then returned to my home and there found my beautiful, lost wife dead.

This is what may transpire when a very bad man tells his very bad master "no."

That was ten years ago. Since that deeply evil day I have endeavored to be a good man. Oh, I know that the stain on my soul can never be fully scoured away, but I tried to slow its spread and lighten its dark ichor with deeds I, perhaps foolishly, deemed good. The Lord knows I tried - if he hasn't abandoned me all together—and I comforted myself in thinking that Miriam, wherever she wandered after death, also knew I tried.

So, in May, knee-deep in flood waters, I found myself looking into the queerly crystal eyes of a man I did not know and heard him tell me that my wife was searching for me from Beyond, and that she was lost. It played well with me superficially, the words like a topical balm, all pleasing and cool to the touch, but I looked at Mount Airy's famous Sgt. Janus and, with the cries and moans of the victims of the flood all around me, asked him what it was that I should do about it. And Sgt. Janus asked me in return to come directly with him to his home and talk to Miriam, to help her find her way.

Standing in the filthy waters which pooled around my legs and my muscles screaming from my exertions, I spoke a word to the Sergeant the likes of which he may or may not have been greatly unfamiliar:

"No."

━╱╲━

Mount Airy Eagle
Early Edition - Tuesday, May 29ᵗʰ

'Spirit-Breaker' Nabs Crooks
Two Persons Accused of Robbery

At approximately 3:40 on the morning of May 29, Mount Airy police officers took one Kenneth Shabbinski of No. 8 Lionel Street into custody. He was subsequently charged at the Jehovah Precinct Station with breaking-and-entering and assault. Mr. Shabbinski was seen to have had bruising on his face and a broken finger on his left hand.

Deputy Police Commissioner Domple reported that officers were called to the Playdium Theater at 1958 Front Street in the early morning hours by a complaint from the owner of a neighboring establishment, the Bells & Whistles. The complaint concerned "strange noises, like moans and shrieks" issuing from the Playdium. The complainant, who had stayed open late for the holiday, said that he knew the Theater had closed for the night and that no such noises should be heard on its premises while not open for business.

Upon entering the premises, the officers encountered one Sgt. Roman Janus of No. 4 Raynham Road who claimed he was "investigating a spirit infestation" at the Playdium. The officers recognized the sergeant as Mount Airy's well-known "spirit-breaker," a reputed hunter of ghosts, and a frequent police consultant. Having determined that Janus was not the source of the reported noises, they were then confronted with Mr. Shabbinski and a lady friend, Miss Adeline Montrose of no fixed address. The gentlemen told the officers that he and Miss Montrose had been imbibing heavily not an hour or so before and that they had "slipped into the Theater for a bit of fun." He further explained that this was the source of the odd sounds heard by the owner of the Bells & Whistles. Sgt. Janus then reportedly informed the officers that Mr. Shabbinski was, in fact, lying and that he was on the premises to rob the Playdium's box office of its receipts. These accusations were supported, said Janus, by "messages from the spirit world," given to the Sergeant on the spot.

Mr. Shabbinski took umbrage to the accusations and assaulted the Sergeant. Before the officers could act, Janus had defended himself and produced bruising on his assailant's face and broken his finger. Mr. Shabbinski was then taken into custody and later charged. Miss Montrose was also apprehended and charged with aiding and abetting. Bail has not yet been set for either of the accused.

After the incident, Sgt. Janus told the police that "the Playdium is a vortex of immeasurable super-natural proportions" and that it "must be sealed off for fear of further spirit infiltration." He also noted that he very strongly believed the recent flood's destruction at the nearby cemetery of St. Barnabas Church was a likely reason for said infiltration. Though reconstruction of the cemetery continues at this time, there have been no disturbances of any kind reported by the priests of the church involving the disturbed graves and mausoleums.

Sgt. Janus could not be reached for further comment on the matter.

—⁄⁄\⌐—

I will explain.

As I have said, I loved my wife and hold myself responsible for her death. Her face still haunts my thoughts, but after ten long years without her I have found something resembling peace over her absence. She led a harsh life, her sanity waxing and waning and her days filled with anxiety and fear, but Miriam is in a better place now; I believe that. I have to believe that. And that is why I told the so-called "spirit-breaker" that, in no uncertain terms, I would not come at his beck and call to fall back into that all-too-familiar spiral of pain and misery.

Miriam - if it were indeed my wife that spoke to Janus—would understand. That, too, I believed.

Janus looked at me with a queer expression on his roughly handsome face, as if noting a glimmer of insanity in my own eyes, but, without further word, he turned on his heel and walked away. I watched his retreat for several minutes then gathered my coat and other things and returned to my simple home, hidden away from the eyes of the world and my former master. Or so I thought.

That was May. I half-expected to hear from Janus again—was he not known to be dogged and persistent in his "crusade" to help those vexed by spirits? How I figured into this profession of his I did not now then, but alas, he did not come 'round again.

That is, until just yesterday when the crisp November air brought a letter from him.

In it, he told me that Miriam had once again made contact with him and that her "misplaced steps are leading her farther and farther into chaos" and I was to come at once to Janus House. After reading the letter one, two, three times, I crumpled it into a ball and flung it into the fire and watched it burn.

I was livid, consumed by rage as I sat there. I was also filled with... dread? For what? I do not know. I had never been afraid of anything before, having lived and worked at the side of a master criminal, but perhaps having subsequently lived with my head down, peering around corners and cloaked in shadows for a decade, had taken its toll with me. But I was also angry, and anger has always fueled me. Oh, yes, a good heated bout of rage can do wonders for my gumption.

I threw on my coat and headed out with Janus House as my destination and murder on my mind.

➤✧◄

The Mount Airy Eagle
Early Edition – Tuesday, June 2nd

About Town with Yours Truly

I can't tell you how simply divine it is to be sitting down with you once again, Dear Readers. And today, though my missive to you is short, I believe it to be exceedingly sweet. Read on!

My travels took me to a very special place yesterday and it's taken me almost a full day to recover from the sojourn. Why, you ask? Surely Yours Truly is made of sterner stuff, not some wilting wallflower who faints at even a hint of toils and travels, eh? Well, Dear Readers, you are correct in that, but this particular journey took me to a destination unlike any Yours Truly has ever visited before: the home of an infamous resident of our little hamlet.

Once inside S.R.J.'s abode – oh, I was chaperoned, have no fear – my eyes were everywhere at once. The outside of the manse is treat enough, if you like an eclectic mix of architecture that appears to be cobbled together from many different and often discordant styles and all that, but the inside…oh my! That defies description, though I will try, Dear Readers; I will try for your precious and curious sakes.

S.R.J. ushered me over the threshold—he's still a bachelor, girls!—and into a pretty little sitting room off the impressive foyer. There, he offered me a luxurious settee on which to set my wondrous little self and once he was settled beside me—oh, golly—we gazed at an immense stone fireplace across the room. Was it romantic, Dear Readers? Propriety keeps me from answering that, you wicked little things…but between you and me, S.R.J. is even more delish up close than he is from afar. If you like the soldier type, that is. I find that I do.

Anyway, while we chatted amiably about a certain charity auction that Yours Truly is heading up in two weeks time—more on that later—I marveled at the unique room's sights and sounds. Oh, yes, sounds! There were sounds galore, from singing off in the distance to the clatter of kitchen utensils and even the whispers of conversations seemingly in other adjoining rooms. But, S.R.J. lives alone, or so we are led to believe! Curiouser and curiouser, Dear Readers, but let's not stop here—read on!

As we spoke on fairly dry matters like objets d'art and such things, my host came over all strangely. Why, at one point I thought he might have drifted off to sleep, a situation that Yours Truly can reassure you,

While we chatted amiably I marveled at the unique room's sights and sounds.

friends, has never happened to the very least of my male companions. Let's be clear on that! But, S.R.J.'s face took on a queer cast, as if he was focused on something far away, something that, well, disturbed him, or at least unsettled him enough to tear his eyes away from my delicious ensemble, Clara Bow eyes and bee-stung lips.

Did we continue talking after that? No, Dear Readers, for my host stood up suddenly, looked around the room, and then reaching out for me took my hand and saw me to the front door of his strange and terrifying house. Terrifying? Yes, in some ways. It had grown darker as we continued our tête-à-tête and settled all over chilly when S.R.J. took notice of something other than Yours Truly. And, incredible though it may sound, several hours had passed while I was there, though it seemed to be only twenty minutes or so!

Astounding, yes? Oh, I know, Dear Readers, I know. I was there.

Still, I don't hold his behavior against him. S.R.J. has always been an odd duck, if I may say so. And I may so because it's my column, right?

Come back tomorrow and we shall speak of other things. Things decidedly warmer, you naughty little boys and girls. You know how it gets around here...

Ta!

—》|《—

It took me until this very morning, almost an entire day, to find a driver who would take me out to Janus House, which sits on the outskirts of Mount Airy.

In that time my anger cooled a bit and I was able to compose myself for the journey – and for facing Janus. I had words for him to hear, and strong ones, but I believed I could deliver them with a relatively rational tongue in my head. After I arrived at the house and began to slog through the mounting snow up the long path to its front door, my anger returned, though, and it was only due to the unexpected sight of the Sergeant himself waiting for me on his front porch that kept me from taking a poke at him.

I opened my mouth to remonstrate Janus for his bothering me with supposed messages from Miriam when he held up one hand, smiled, and then reached out to take my own hand in greeting. Something about his demeanor brought me up short and I meekly shook his offered hand. Nodding silently, he ushered me inside Janus House as if he and I were old friends.

The insides of his mansion were dark. I didn't know what to expect, having heard many wild tales of the mansion's particulars, and I could make out precious little in the gloom to confirm or deny them. Janus explained that the house was being "cleaned" and seemed to think that a sound enough reason for the darkness. I turned to him in the shadowy foyer and demanded to know why he persisted in approaching me about Miriam.

"She is lost, as I have endeavored to tell you," he said simply. "Your wife is quite lost and even my own abilities are not enough to shed enough light to illuminate the path to her designated resting place."

Before I could speak again, he continued. "You see," he whispered, nodding, "her mind has not healed, even beyond the grave, as is customary. It was…shredded when she was very young, and the damage was of an extent that it was a wonder she was able to function at all into adulthood. Perhaps some credit for that was due to your very great love and depth of feeling for her."

I was stunned. I came to Janus House with thoughts of malice in my head and here the Sergeant had defused me completely with just a few words. Knocked back on my heels, I stammered out a reply.

"Shredded?" I asked, confused. "By what?"

"Spirits," said Janus, his cool eyes searching mine. "Selfish, vengeful spirits…"

Sandor,

I have arrived in Mount Airy and have taken a room at a small inn near the center of town. Amazingly, there are little to no signs of the flooding, despite it being only two months after the event. To their credit, the townspeople have managed to rebuild their home in record time.

Once settled and waiting a day before venturing out, I walked to the cemetery. It is just as we had heard—all praise The Nameless One! Perhaps now, finally, we may begin the rites, after all this time.

The ground there is level, though I suspect it was not so before the flood. Few stones remain and those that do are for the most part still not set to right. Only one mausoleum is standing – the name on it is "Yanuse" – but I could see the foundations of at least six more. There are open graves – all praise He Who Waits!

As I walked the perimeter of the cemetery, I grew emboldened, forgive me, and approached a priest who was drifting among the plots. He was a wretched sort, all smiles and rosy cheeks and a twinkle in his eyes, and it was all I could do not to strike him down where he stood. Instead, I asked of the recovery of the site and he happily informed me of the church's operations. The man grew even more gregarious when I hinted that I might lean toward a charitable donation to their efforts.

I left him to go about his duties—whatever those were—and left the cemetery. Later, after sunset, I returned to the grounds and gathered samples of grave soil and a few bits of broken tombstone—all praise The Multi-Horned Ram!

When I feel that the time is right, I will begin to impede the church's progress and perhaps even murder one of the priests. That may help in the rites, though I admit it's a bit theatrical.

One more thing, Sandor: there are other forces at work here, one of them benevolent and the other most infernal. Alas, I can say no more on this for I have not determined the exact nature of either, except to say the former is very well entrenched here and the latter has only recently sent its tendrils into the earth around Mount Airy. We should move carefully and avoid confrontation with any other sects, of course, especially one that exhibits the peculiar strength which I have sensed from this one.

I will write again soon.

Your brother in the name of The Eternal Conflagration,
Rator

—⟩⟨—

Before I could ask Janus to clarify his bold statement, he took me by the arm and led me through an ornate archway and down a darkened hallway. Dumbfounded, I went along with him without protest, my mind chewing on his allegations of Miriam's early life.

Finally, after a lengthy walk through darkened corridors and gloomy rooms, I could make out a small sliver of light coming from under a doorway up ahead of us. The Sergeant stopped in front of that door, held out a hand for me to pause, and then stood silently for a moment. He seemed to be listening for something. I myself heard nothing. Then, somehow satisfied, he turned the knob and opened the door. Light flooded into the hallway and he motioned for me to enter the room beyond.

I stepped into a space that, had my mood been more cheerful, I might have called charming. It was decorated tastefully, with a fine balance between the male and female sensibilities and with a small, crackling fire in its ornate brick fireplace. There was one window, but its shades and curtains were drawn tight and, interestingly, the only furniture present and of note were two chairs, both of them comfortable-looking and facing each other in roughly the center of the room.

I turned to look at Janus, unsure of what exactly I was to make of it all.

"The Room of Visitation welcomes you," he said plainly and without flourish, and insisted I sit down in one of the chairs, whichever one I chose. He himself swiveled on his heel and made as to exit the room.

Well, I had no intention of "visiting" long with the man and told him that to be called to his home and then shuffled off into a parlor while he did God Knows What was simply not on my agenda. I demanded to be told what he knew of my wife in resolute fashion.

Janus' frowned slightly, shook his head, and then asked me once again to sit down. All would be explained soon, he said. The Lord only knows why, but I did as he asked. A moment later and he had left the room.

Sitting in one of the chairs, I began to feel foolish. I looked around the damnable room and realized how ridiculous it all was, how it seemed to be a charade of some sort and that I had fallen into the hands of a lunatic. I moved to stand up.

I heard a door open. I looked up at the only door in the room, but it remained as it was after Janus had left; closed and silent. There was no other door into the room; I was certain of it.

Then someone stepped around from behind me, behind my chair, and, with a displacement of air and a rustle of cloth, sat down in the chair opposite me.

It was Miriam.

—✦—

The Riddleton Tribune
Morning Edition – November 1st, 1899

Child Abducted from Home

A female child of undetermined age was taken from her family home at approximately midnight on October 31ˢᵗ, in the Bertswa neighborhood. Commissioner of Police Fenton reports that little else is known about the incident and that no clues exist as to her abductors or her current whereabouts. In addition, he was reluctant to release the child's name until the matter had been settled to his satisfaction.

Strange figures had been seen in the vicinity of the home by neighbors, though officials deny those reports. An eyewitness that asked to remain anonymous said that "queer-eyed gipsies" crossed his own lawn on the afternoon of October 31ˢᵗ, and that they "smelled of trouble." The man claimed to have chased the persons from his property with a shotgun, but that he had heard from another neighbor that the mysterious figures returned some hours later at dusk.

The location of these foreign individuals is not known at this time.

Commissioner Fenton added to his statement, under duress, that no request for ransom has yet been delivered to either the child's family or the police.

—⁄∣⁀—

This next movement in my story is difficult to contemplate, let alone to put down on paper, but I feel it is important that others know of it, though it is extremely personal, so that they may make up their own minds as to the truth of it…or the lie.

My lovely, lost Miriam sat before me in that room. Janus had somehow conjured her up, in every last detail, and before my very eyes. I rose out of my chair to approach her, but she raised one pale, slim hand to caution me against doing so.

"You cannot embrace me, Thomas," she said, her voice like a whisper. "That is no longer possible."

I asked her why that was, though I knew in my heart that the gulf between us was now wide and impossible to cross. She smiled thinly and sadly, as if in answer, and urged me to speak no more on that particular matter. It was as it was; she was beyond mortal comforts.

"I am lost, Thomas!" she suddenly wailed, and I steeled myself against the emotions flooding through me—it looked, sounded so much like Miriam! As God is my witness, I swear it was truly her! Before I could do or say anything, she continued in a calmer voice.

"I am plagued here as I was in life – I do not know which way to turn, as there seems to be no true directions here. There is little to distinguish left from right, up from down…even right from wrong. Oh, it is more a nightmare than eternal rest…"

I wondered what sort of Deity would allow this to happen to someone like Miriam. Was this what we were promised by the clergy, by the Good

Book? My wife suffered so in life; was she to be tormented in death, too? I swore out loud, looked around the room for something to break, but, calming myself, asked her what I could do for her.

"Release me," she whispered, her eyes searching mine. "Release me…"

I felt as lost then as Miriam. Untold frustrations bubbled up, and an utter feeling of helplessness took hold of me with an iron grip. I opened my mouth to speak.

"Someone is coming!" said Miriam abruptly, the same look of madness in her eyes I came to fear while she lived.

"Thomas, Thomas! Help me! He is coming for me!"

⸺⸌⟋⟍⸍⸺

The Fortescu Times
February 1993 – Vol. 1, No. 142

Janus Speaks!
The Sergeant in his Own Words
By J. Reynolds

Recently, the former Mount Airy Eagle building was purchased by Trans-Global Media Partners and cleared for demolition. Documents dating back to the mid-1800s were discovered in the basement of the building and among them this curious document. It appears to be a transcription of an interview by an Eagle staff writer and Sgt. Roman Janus, the infamous Spirit-Breaker of the early 20th century, conducted on an unknown date.

The Eagle ran a regular column called "The Professional Corner," in which it published interviews with various people of different professions in an effort to illuminate business concerns and other related interests—the column featured two writers, Cortland Smith and Norman Prapp, but I've been unable to determine which of the men conducted the following interview. I have been able to confirm that it was never published, though we don't know why, and I assume it would have been edited into prose fashion rather than the question-and-answer format you see here.

The interview offers a rare and somewhat candid viewpoint on the enigmatic Roman Janus, especially on the subject of why a Supreme Being would oversee a spirits and hauntings. The Fortescu Times is very happy to be able to present it to you.

"Someone is coming!"

Interviewer: Please state your name and profession.

Janus: I am Sgt. Roman E. Janus, Spirit-Breaker.

Interviewer: Could you be more precise, sir, in your profession?

Janus: Certainly. I aid those who are troubled by the supernatural.

Interviewer: Quite. And in what sorts of forms may the 'supernatural' assume to trouble people?

Janus: Oh, well, far too many, to be sure. I generally weigh in on matters of hauntings and other such spectral or near-spectral visitations, but I also have been known to consult and take a more direct hand in possessions, both of humans and of inanimate objects. I rarely turn anyone away who comes to me with a worrisome problem of a psychical nature.

Interviewer: Would you say that there are many people you meet in your trade who do not believe in the supernatural or ghosts?

Janus: Yes, and I very much sympathize with them. The etheric world has yet to fully capture the attention and belief of the general populace, and, if I might say so, I almost envy them that ignorance. It is not an easy life, that of a Spirit-Breaker, and there are days when I would just as soon pick up a good book and a nice brandy than banish another arduous spirit.

Interviewer: You say 'has yet to fully capture' – do you mean, sir that…well, that seems to indicate something rather ominous on the horizon for mankind.

Janus: I humbly apologize if I alarmed you. What I mean to say is that the connection between the waking world and the spirit plane has grown closer over the past several hundred years and will continue to do so, but it will be several more centuries before any possibility of full juxtaposition. You and I shall be long into dust by then. Have no fear.

Interview: Well, then, how do you 'break' these spirits? Do you utilize more than one way of interjecting yourself into these…these 'situations'?

Janus: Generally, it's a matter of spotting the connection point and analyzing its nature. From there I choose from several different, ah, surgical strikes to sever the ties between the spirits and the living. And not all of them are of a violent bent. Sometimes, the kid glove is just as effective as the saber. The intention is to send the dead on their proper way, along the path that was always meant for them. For the most part, the spirits are not entirely responsible for their earthly imprisonment or the pain and suffering that often comes along with it. *Such souls need to be shown the door with dignity and decorum.*

Interviewer: *But there are those spirits that have been, shall we say, reluctant to heed your direction?*

Janus: *Yes. Rather a lot, really. Those cases I must approach more forcefully, and, yes, even violently. It is a strange business sometimes.*

Interviewer: *I should say so. It boggles the mind. Why would such an injustice exist? It seems a poor way to run a universe, if the Almighty will forgive me for saying so.*

Janus: *More than a few people have remarked upon that to me throughout my career, and I tell them all the same thing—I cannot speak for the Deity and His purposes and His reasoning. I am but His humble servant and operate as I see fit to set the system right when it goes wrong.*

Interviewer: *Then you are a religious man, sir?*

Janus: *Well, what is religion, exactly? A system, like many others, of course, beset by rules and regulations, but with the object of bringing peace and happiness under Our Lord here on Earth. I do not subscribe to any organized church or services, but practice a religion of one: myself. Some may not see it as a religion, but again I ask you: what is religion?*

Interviewer: *We would not presume to debate you on that score, so let us move on. You have published several books on the subject of the supernatural and spiritualism, each one of them entirely unlike any other authors' volumes on the like. Are you working on anything at the moment? Will we be seeing your memoirs before long?*

Janus: *Memoirs are for the dead, or the near-dead. If I should ever be moved to write such a book or set of books, I will wait until after I am long departed. For the here and now, I am currently toiling on a volume I shall title "The Ghost of Sumatra," which will detail a most fascinating case, one of the most unique of my career to date. When it will be finished, I cannot say, for there are certain aspects of the case that continue to this day.*

Interviewer: *Sgt. Janus, you run your operation with no partners, no employees, and, if I am not mistaken, you are not a married man. Is there anyone in your life at this time, a special someone, someone who perhaps understands your profession and could possibly even aid you in it?*

Janus: *Ah, look at the time. I'm afraid this has taken a bit longer than I expected. Thank you very much for having me and please send*

me a note when the article will be published. I will look forward to it.
Good day, sir.
   Interviewer: *And to you, sir, a very good day. Thank you.*

My poor wife's desperate plea shocked me, horrified me. I didn't know what to do, helpless as I was to affect the spirit world, but before I could speak and somehow assuage her anxiety, the door to the room was suddenly flung open. There in the doorway stood Sgt. Janus.

"Thomas," he said tersely, "I seem to have uninvited guests. Please come with me."

My only thought was for Miriam, but when I looked from the Sergeant back to her, she was gone. Completely gone, as if she was never there. My heart instantly ached for her, to see her face again.

Shaking it off, I rose from my chair and followed Janus out of the room and down the darkened hallway beyond. I asked him what was the matter, who he spoke of. He urged me to stay quiet and soon we approached the foyer to his home, where I had entered Janus House seemingly hours before. We came upon the area through a door that opened up beside his grand staircase and immediately I heard loud banging at his front door. Janus motioned for me to stop with a quick snap of his hand. The pounding increased and we heard a man's loud bellowing, demanding to be let in.

"You have something that belongs to our employer," the man outside growled. Incredibly, the voice was familiar to me.

Wordlessly, the Sergeant attracted my attention and pointed off to the right; a clear sign that he wanted me to vacate to a side room. Something in his silent command led me to obey and I slipped though the doorway he indicated and hid myself behind some drapery near the entrance. This afforded me some view of the foyer. Looking over to Janus, I found he had vanished, but his departing words still hung in the air around me.

"Wait—and watch."

The front door burst open with a resounding explosion. The glass in its windows shattered and splinters of wood flew across the foyer to impact the doorframe opposite it. Loathsome, dark figures occupied the open doorway, silhouetted in the remaining sunlight of the day. With calm bravado, they entered Janus House, their shoes crunching bits of glass as they did. The first man stopped abruptly when he reached the foyer, pointing.

I followed his finger to the staircase and was amazed at what I saw there.

A large transparent form was floating down the grand staircase, silent and unearthly. As it neared the mid-point, I thought it took on a more… human design; fantastic, but chilling. Beyond that I cannot say more other than noting a soft wailing that issued from it.

I tore my eyes from the ghastly thing and looked back to the intruders; they had paused, Oriental eyes wide, mouths hanging open on otherwise-cruel faces. Surely they would bolt, I thought; I myself was fighting the urge to rabbit away from the scene. But, they held their ground and the lead man slipped a pistol from his jacket, pointed it at the apparition, and pulled the trigger.

The others with him followed suit.

They were hardened men. Precious little in Heaven and on Earth could cause fear in them for more than a moment. I knew this because I knew them, all too well.

—✠—

Official Report of Deputy James A. McPeek
Badge #4, Mount Airy Police Department

On July 3rd of this year I was Ordered to begin to Surveil the Activities of an individual believed to be part of a Larger Criminal Group. This group has been known to hold rites of a diabolic nature and to be heavily Involved in the illicit narcotic trade as well as perhaps white slavery.

The individual, called Rator, though I Discovered his Real Name to be Robert Roth, has taken a room at the Burgess Inn on Gregg Street and uses it as a base of Operations. At least once a week Roth writes a letter to an assumed compatriot in another town and mails it at the Gregg Street station. I have failed to this date to intercept any of these letters.

Roth has made at least seven trips to the cemetery of St. Barnabas Church Since his arrival in Mount Airy. One these occasions he has removed both soil and pieces of masonry from the premises, which he stores in his room at the inn. He is careful and meticulous with them, though I do not yet know for what purpose he does this.

On at least three occasions he has spoken with Father Harold of St. Barnabas, and on the latest of these meetings sat down for tea with the priest. At that meeting, I witnessed Roth pour out his tea while the Father was not looking.

On July 13th, I was able to search Roth's room while he was away at the cemetery. This was done with the full permission of the inn's owner and manager. Among Roth's possessions I discovered books and pamphlets on the subject of diabolism, human sacrifice, narcotic production, and one volume with pictures of a sensitive nature involving children. I removed nothing from the room, but left it exactly as I found it.

Roth has also entertained prostitutes in his room on at least seven occasions, each of which roughly Corresponds to his trips to the cemetery. One such woman has filed a complaint on the man at our precinct building for his overly-rough treatment of her during their tryst.

In summation, I submit that Robert Roth is planning a larger criminal campaign in Mount Airy, most likely concerning his group of diabolists and the cemetery at St. Barnabas. He is about this at his leisure; therefore I can only surmise that this supposed event will not take place until the fall.

Furthermore, I have found no evidence to link Roth and his group to the other criminal activity that our department has taken notice of recently in Mount Airy. As we know, that cabal is made up primarily of oriental nationals and seems to be operating in the denser areas of our town. Though there is the Similarity of the drug trade between Roth and this other group, I have uncovered no ctual narcotic movement from Roth to this date.

This ends my report. Until such time that you recall me, I shall continue to investigate Robert Roth and his activities.

━╱╲━

Things happened at a rapid pace after that. Having recognized the men as former colleagues of mine, I attempted to parlay with them. That was a mistake. My edge in dealing with such matters had obviously grown dull after ten years of hiding from my old master.

Still, the sight of me stepping out of the ante-room was enough to put an end to their shooting at the ghostly figure coming down the stairs. It disappeared as quickly as it appeared and Sgt. Janus came down the stairs in its place, frowning at the men.

I asked them what they wanted. To my surprise, they wanted me and not Miriam.

"You have been away for far too long, Thomas," said the leader, who I knew as Cho-Soung. "He requires your presence once more at his side. Ten years is long enough for you to have been reacquainted with the notion of freedom—but, as you well know, freedom is an illusion. We are here to bring you back to where you belong, to he who owns you, body and soul."

Sgt. Janus said nothing, but I could feel both strength and a calming air emanate from him, helping me to face the intruders in his home. I stammered out Miriam's name, asking what part she played in it all. The Cho-Soung laughed, a cruel sound to my ears.

"Your wife?" His brow creased in slight confusion. "Why, Thomas, no part at all. She has played her part long ago. He is quite done with her."

"You mean her death?" I spat at him, the pain from her murder still a dull ache in my heart, even after all these years.

"No," he replied, "her life."

"I think I begin to see it," said Sgt. Janus, stepping up beside me, placing a firm, steadying hand on my shoulder. "Your master is responsible for the spirits that drove her to the edge of madness."

The man nodded matter-of-factly, looking upon us as if we were children who had stumbled upon a fact that everyone else already knew.

"A portal," continued Janus grimly. "A gate. A spirit-gate. She told me as much, but I did not understand at the time. Your master used her natural talents as a spirit-gate when she was a child to converse with the dead. And for the rest of her life she paid the toll for his...his bloody crime."

"How dare he?"

Suddenly Janus' voice was as loud as a hundred voices, all shouting at once. It rocked me backwards, almost off my feet.

My former colleagues did not fare as well; they were sent sprawling, bowled end over end. The walls shook, the ceiling swayed, plaster fell, somewhere a window cracked and shattered. The reverberations from the shout lasted for a full minute—my ears ached for hours afterwards.

Janus came rushing upon them where they lay like a banshee. Looming over the three men, it seemed as if he was sucking all the light out of the air and into himself. I could not see his countenance, for he was facing them and away from me, but it must have been horrible indeed: their own faces were twisted into masks of fear and loathing.

"I have a message for your doctor," Janus bellowed, deep and sonorous. "Oh yes, I know who he is, as I have been watching the devil from the corners of my eyes for many years. From this moment on I shall have *all* of my eyes upon him and all that he does.

"Tell him this is finished. Tell him that Thomas Tan and his wife are under my care."

The men's faces blanched. They scrambled to their feet and backed away from Janus, visibly shaking. Finally, they were through the door and gone from our sight. Janus issued one last message, this time as a whisper:

"And tell your doctor that he shall pay one day for his heinous crime…"

I sat there for what seemed an eternity. The sun set and still I continued to sit. Much later, Sgt. Janus appeared at my side once more and crouched down to force me to look him in the eye.

"Come, Thomas," he said kindly. "Miriam awaits you. You must now free her."

My dearest, lovely Thomas,

I write this on the occasion of our wedding, a day I have longed for since the moment I met you and one I will cherish all my remaining days.

I must write this now, while I still feel myself. Though in a matter of a few short hours we shall be married, there are things I wish to set down now, so that later, when I may not feel well, you may read them and know my true thoughts.

You have become my family, my darling, for I have had none previously. For this I shall be eternally grateful to you. Whatever life I led before this day, whatever I may have done, it is all behind me. Nothing matters more than our life together beyond this day.

You have cared for me when I have been ill and you have promised to care for me in the future. This means more to me than you can ever know, for it speaks of your unending capacity for sympathy and love, to take pity on me and my strange ways. For this you have sacrificed some of your freedom, though I know that you say it is not so. I know better, you see, for I know your heart and you mine.

I do not ask you to tell me of your life, of the things you do to provide for us and keep us safe and sound. That is your business and I as a good wife will never question it. You do what you see as right and I will forever be there to welcome you home each day. When it is dark, I will be your light. When you require solace, I will provide it without question.

"Come, Thomas, Miriam awaits you."

There is one thing I ask of you, on those nights when we will lie together as husband and wife and I am myself: do not ask me of my memories before we met. You have seen my pain, glimpsed it on many occasions, and you have remained silent. Please, my dearest one, hold that silence, I beg of you.

Someday, when the last trumpet sounds and we look upon each other on another plane, deep in the arms of our Creator, then we shall talk of many things. Until then, know that I love you and that I am devoted to you and that beyond my illness stands a woman who is yours forever more.
Eternally,
Miriam

―✸―

As we raced through the darkened corridors of Janus House back to the Room of Visitation, I asked Janus how it was that my former employer and his servants knew of my poor Miriam—as far as I could determine, he had never met my wife nor gleaned her existence.

"He may have been manipulating events all along," said the Sergeant with a heavy sigh. "For years, in fact. He may have arranged for you to meet Miriam, for some nefarious purposes of his own. I have a good friend in the constabulary who will look into it if I ask him to…he and the Doctor have met before.

"Now, here we are at the Room once again. Miriam needs you, Thomas. Apparently, an old link still exists between the Doctor and her—you must stand between them and break that link."

"With what?" I asked.

"With your great love for her," he replied.

I think, at that moment, that I began to understand a small portion of what it is exactly that Sgt. Janus does. With his unswerving love for humanity, he breaks the ties between here and…the other place, and sends souls onward to their true rest. But though I was filled with that revelation, my frustration over being manipulated for years remained hot in my blood.

"Why did Miriam not tell me?"

Janus looked upon me kindly. "She could not. Her madness, you see. It must have been Hell on Earth for her, but now, you have the opportunity to right that terrible wrong."

He opened the door to the Room and we both stepped inside. It was exactly the same as I had left it. Moving across the Room I immediately took the chair that I had vacated only an hour before and looked up at Janus for direction. He seemed pleased that I needed no urging to proceed.

"Miriam will come to you once more," he said, moving about the Room and touching several objects, seemingly making minute adjustments to them, perhaps not unlike tuning a radio. "You are the key to her imprisonment. You are the light she will follow to find her way back to the path."

I told him that Miriam had always said she was *my* light.

Smiling sadly, he walked behind my chair and out of my view. I heard a door open, much as I had before in the Room, but again I wondered at that—there was no other door save the one that I could plainly see, the one through which we had come not minutes before.

Then, Miriam sat before me again, this time not taking the chair opposite me, but kneeling at my feet, her head resting upon my knee and one hand stroking my leg. Oh, I nearly cried with anguish!

"Now, Thomas," came the voice of Sgt. Janus, bodiless and ghost-like, "break the link."

"But how?" I wailed, feeling the madness that crawled through Miriam in life, now through her shade that sat before of me, lovely in its form. I wanted to reach out and touch her, but I remembered what she had said before: I could not physically embrace her.

"Part of you still works for *him*. Reject it. Reject him. Break the link."

I looked down at my wife, my poor, lost Miriam. My feelings for her were clear, clear as cut crystal. My feelings toward my former master were clear—or so I thought. I believed that I had cut my ties with him ten years ago, but I saw then that all I had severed was what existed in the material world. My soul still rested in his hands.

Drawing on my still-heated love for Miriam, I reached out with my mind and cut the ties. I broke the link.

"Miriam!" I cried out. "He cannot—will not—hurt you further! I will not allow it!"

Janus' voice filled the room, strength in audible form.

"Go thee to thy rest, oh shade. Thou hast served well in life, now take thy reward…"

Unable to control myself anymore, I reached out to touch Miriam, but she was gone.

And, I knew with a certainty, no longer lost.

I sat for a long time in that chair in the Room of Visitation, a part of me hoping that her ghost would return to me, somehow. Then, after many hours, I got up and rejoined Janus in his front parlor. When he saw me enter the area, he smiled and clapped me on the back, his sympathy evident despite his lack of words. I thanked him and told him I should be finding my way home, though I was unsure how I would achieve that goal, being without a motorcar or other transportation.

In the end, the Sergeant insisted that I borrow his own auto. He made his apologies for not accompanying me, but he needed to stay at the house and continue to supervise its "cleaning." He would send someone around later to pick up his car.

The car turned out to be a brand-new Hudson Phaeton. Driving it served to alleviate some of my depression.

As I rode along, down the long drive from Janus House and then turning onto Raynham Road, I looked out at the beautiful snow all around me and finally felt free. Free for the first time in decades, since my childhood to be precise. I felt as if a heavy burden had been lifted off of me and that I could finally breathe.

It was over.

Or so I thought right up until the very second the other car appeared out of nowhere and crashed into me, sending the Phaeton tumbling over and over and down into a ditch…

22 November

I have sent my servants to attend to the matter of Tan, though they have not yet returned from that task. I have readied my laboratory for surgery in anticipation of their arrival. In the meantime I have turned to other matters that require my attention.

The diabolists have been dealt with, as children are dealt with by a parent. They sought to mask their presence in this town from me, but their actions were clumsy and juvenile. Their cult was still young, though they felt as if though they had toiled at their preparations for a lifetime. In the end its destruction was simple and with little effort on my part. The local police force will find their agent's corpse soon and the priests of St. Barnabas will find a tidy sum in their tithing box.

I must commend the diabolists on one score, though; they have illuminated a source of great occult strength in this area of the country, one of which I had not previously been aware. The great flood of earlier in the year brought about some change or alteration to the Hidden World on this plane and in this town. My attention has now been brought to it and I will proceed in identifying it further.

This one called Janus intrigues me. His past is shrouded to me currently, but I have been able to discern some ability in him, a connection to the Hidden World that presently defies explanation, though I concede that it may simply be attributed to narcotics and pharmaceuticals. He refers to himself as a "spirit-breaker"—I am unaware of this term, though further research may yet turn up the meaning behind it. For the moment, Janus exists as a point of interest, nothing more. Should he meddle in my affairs or otherwise concern himself in my activities, then I shall devote more attention to him.

My servants return. I go now to welcome Tan back into my good graces, though there will be, of course, a price he pays for my forgiveness.

—✦—

I am very good at eluding people.

After I was flung from the automobile its fuel tank ruptured and caught fire. The fire covered my tracks, allowing me to crawl through the snow and rest here under the Raynham Road Bridge. The falling snow, now quite heavy, has also served to hide me.

My attackers most likely believed I was dead, trapped in the burning wreckage, but now that the fire has receded they have found no body and are most certainly hunting me once again. I have gained enough time to write this record, but I'm afraid that time is now slipping away, signaling the final act of this little drama.

My old master does not let go of things easily, it seems.

The pain is now excruciating. My heart is behaving strangely; perhaps it will give out before they find me. That would be a blessing.

I am at peace, oh yes! With Miriam safe I can finally rest. No more running, no more hiding, no more looking over my shoulder. I'll face those I've hurt in my life and make my apologies.

Hard to write.

My plan is to place this record somewhere safe, somewhere beyond the reach of the hunters. I hope I can still achieve that—Janus at least will find it of some significance, I'm sure.

I hope.

It has been a long journey, and a strange one.

Ah, the pain! I must stop writing now can barely hold the pencil. Hear someone coming. Wait. There, over the field over the snow.

Miriam.

Miriam walking across the snow barefoot in summer dress I bought her so long ago. She said it was too daring too breezy too much like someone else might wear.

She looked lovely in it. She *looks* lovely in it.

Her skin radiant. Her smile—oh Lord! Her smile. I had forgotten…

Someone behind her walking with her—Janus? No, gone now.

I am gone

Miriam sweet Miriam her smile kissing me taking paper from my hand

Yes

—⁂—

The Mount Airy Eagle
Late Edition – Thursday, November 23rd

Man Found Dead Outside of Town
Body Discovered Near Wrecked Automobile

Early this morning, police found the body of a man who had seemingly crawled from the wreckage of an automobile near the Raynham Road Bridge.

The body was that of a man of mixed Caucasian and Oriental ancestry, approximately thirty-five-years-old and in sound health, and dressed in a dark suit and coat of good quality. There were no apparent wounds from the crash, said a representative from the Mount Airy Coroner's office, though he had been deceased for some hours. He has not yet been identified, due to the lack of possessions of any kind on his person, save for a well-used pencil found in his hand.

No residents of Raynham Road nor of the surrounding area of come forward to offer information on the either the crash or the dead man, said Deputy Police Commissioner Domple.

"We are canvassing the neighborhood," he reported. "Any individuals with any information should come forward, as is their duty as citizens of Mount Airy. This is a serious matter."

When asked if the automobile's owner was known, the Deputy Police Commissioner noted that it was registered to Sgt. Roman Janus of No. 4 Raynham Road, but that the man had not yet been found for questioning. The automobile was a Hudson Phaeton and only a year

old and in good repair before the crash.

Deputy Police Commissioner Domple was also asked if he believed the event had any connection with the increase of criminal activity of late in Mount Airy, but he declined to comment on that score.

THE END

CALLING SGT. JANUS!

When the invitation to become part of this collection arrived, not only was I honored to be asked, but in some ways it made me feel like Sgt. Janus had "arrived." How so, you ask? Hasn't he—at the time I write this—enjoyed two whole volumes of his adventures? Yes, but this book marks his first venture alongside his esteemed colleagues—I'd like to think that it's a sign of Sgt. Janus acceptance as a peer to the world's greatest modern occult detectives.

It's fascinating to me how a small sub-category of Pulp Hero has been taken up by modern writers and not only kept breathing, but infinitely expanded upon, Not content with simply hiking the same paths as such scribes as William Hope Hodgson, Seabury Quinn, Algernon Blackwood, Manly Wade Wellman, etc., new writers are finding new ways to present the Occult Detective trope and thrill an entire new generation with it.

Personally, I couldn't be more excited by it all. And this volume is proof that I'm not the only one who feels that way.

So, editor Ron Fortier asked me for a new Sgt. Janus tale, but I was a little crushed for time and proposed something else. Over at the Official Sgt. Janus Spirit-Blog (www.sgtjanus.blogspot.com), I'd serialized a Janus story in ten installments and readers seemed to like it. My suggestion to Ron was that I'd take that and expand it to double its length by adding all-new material and sprucing up the rest. He gave me an enthusiastic "Yes!" and I got to work on what would be the very first Janus story to seek its fortunes outside of his own bailiwick.

"The Lost Wife of Thomas Tan" originally detailed the macabre events surrounding the title character to pierce the mystery of his late wife and his efforts to elude his former employer. I liked that story, but as I examined it from all angles I realized that Thomas had said everything I wanted him to say and that I didn't want to disturb what I felt was a solid "done-in-one." What to do with it then? Then it came to me: there must be other stories going on all around him; why not find one of those?

SGT. JANUS, SPIRIT-BREAKER used a device wherein different narrators—Janus clients—relate their own stories in their own voices. This was something I came up with to give the reader multiple perspectives on the Sergeant and his world, and to help me "get over" my own dislike for first-person narratives in fiction. At the Spirit-Blog, I went a bit farther with it and included dispatches from a local newspaper in Janus' neck of the woods and had a good time with it. That was the key, I felt, to lengthening "The Lost Wife of Thomas Tan."

In the end, I hope the story imparts something of the structure of Bram Stoker's legendary novel DRACULA, with its make-up of journal entries and other such personal and public writings. The adventures of Sgt. Janus are all about experimentation, as far as I'm concerned, and I am grateful not only for the opportunity to indulge myself in that vein for this collection, but also to you, the reader, for your time and interest in my character, my ode to all the other Occult Detectives who have come before.

And, if your interest still holds, Sgt. Janus will return in the full-length novel SGT. JANUS ON THE DARK TRACK, upcoming from Airship 27.

Now, excuse me; someone seems to have sent me a rather exotic-looking giant centipede...I wonder who that could be?

JIM BEARD - A native Toledoan, Jim Beard was introduced to comic books at an early age by his father, who passed on to him a love for the medium and the pulp characters who preceded it. After decades of reading, collecting and dissecting comics, Jim became a published writer when he sold a story to DC Comics in 2002. Since that time he's written official Star Wars and Ghostbusters comic stories and contributed articles and essays to several volumes of comic book history.

His work includes GOTHAM CITY 14 MILES, a book of essays on the 1966 Batman TV series; SGT. JANUS, SPIRIT-BREAKER, a collection of pulp ghost stories featuring his own Edwardian occult detective; CAPTAIN ACTION: RIDDLE OF THE GLOWING MEN, the first pulp prose novel based on the classic 1960s action figure; and MONSTER EARTH, a shared-world anthology of giant monster tales.

Currently, Jim provides regular content for Marvel.com, the official Marvel Comics website, is a regular columnist for Toledo Free Press and has forthcoming comic and prose work from Bluewater, TwoMorrows, Airship 27 and Pro Se.

Please visit him at http://sgtjanus.blogspot.com and on Facebook at http://facebook.com/thebeardjimbeard

JAZZY

BY RON FORTIER

Ravenwood poured cream into his coffee and watched it transform the hot black liquid into swirling pool of a soft brown color. It reminded him immediately of his mother's eyes; one of the few lasting memories he had of her. She and his father had died when he was a small child in the Orient. Medical missionaries, they had been treating villagers in a plague-ridden locale when they both succumbed to the disease.

The memory was a cherished one. Tender brown eyes that had showered love on him for too short a time.

Ravenwood stirred the coffee with his spoon and then took a slow sip. The taste was both hardy and smooth; delicious as ever. He surveyed his surroundings. Of all the mysteries in the universe, this had the be the most puzzling; that the best coffee in all of New York City was to be had in a greasy-spoon diner called MURPHY'S on the west side of 7ᵗʰ Avenue several blocks south of Times Square.

It was after two in the morning and the place was deserted except for Jake, an old Negro short-order cook, and Wanda, a heavy-set brunette waitress who occupied her time doing crossword puzzles at the far end of the counter. Jake, for the most part, stayed busy baking pastries in the back kitchen; from bagels to donuts. These were all intended for the breakfast crowd who would daily invade the small, rectangular shaped eatery at the first light of dawn.

Ravenwood had discovered the diner years earlier upon his return home; a wealthy young man about to launch his career as an Occult Investigator. So much had happened since then, arriving back in America with his Tibetan mentor, the wise and mysterious monk he knew only as the Nameless One. Shortly thereafter he'd hired Sterling; the British gentlemen's gentlemen and gourmet chef to oversee his swank, Manhattan penthouse suite. In the past decade, he and his two associates had confronted all manner of bizarre occurrences; fought both human and demonic monsters while at the same time protecting the blissfully ignorant citizens of their wonderful city.

We're a strange family, we three. Ravenwood smiled at his own musings and started to take another drink of his rich coffee.

The door to the diner banged open and two customers entered; swept in by a cool gust of air. The first was a young girl with midnight black hair that was tied in a ponytail and half hidden beneath a man's woolen cap tucked down to hide her face. Ravenwood guessed her to be fifteen or sixteen whereas the person behind her was taller and older. This one, also female, wore a heavy black cloak and hood with black leather gloves and carried a worn, brown carpetbag that looked heavy. He assumed she was the girl's mother.

"Gosh, it's bloody cold out there," the teenager said as she beat her own gloved hands together.

She had a European accent with a strong Germanic flavor. Perhaps, Austria…or Transylvania. Ravenwood continued to enjoy his coffee while at the same time mentally sizing up these late night women.

"Springtime in the big city," Wanda explained as she stepped forward with two well-worn menus in her hand. "Would you girls like a booth or you can sit up at the counter." She waved her hand at the near empty interior. "Wherever is fine with me."

At that the woman reached up and pulled the hood off her head.

Ravenwood's breath caught in his throat as her beautiful face was revealed. She possessed an old world classical beauty of smooth alabaster skin with fine chiseled features, full red lips, a sharp Roman nose and dark, delicately shaped eyebrows over two large eyes. Her hair, like her daughter's, was jet black with a few streaks of gray peeking through. It was shoulder length and appeared uncombed.

He sensed an unsettling urgency about her.

In the process of lowering her hood, the woman had turned her head to survey their surroundings and for a fleeting second her eyes locked with his. Even from this distance their vibrant jade green color shined.

"A booth will do nicely, thank you." Her voice was cultured, confident and mature.

Wanda started to usher them towards the area where Ravenwood was seated when the woman stopped her. "Perhaps a booth to our right so as to not disturb the gentlemen's privacy."

Wanda shrugged her shoulders and turned on her heels. "No problem, dearie. Just you and your girl pick out whatever booth you'd like."

The woman nodded and followed her but not before glancing at Ravenwood one final time. He smiled demurely and nodded acknowledging her thoughtfulness for which he received a guarded smile in return. Although appreciating her gesture he suddenly felt as if he'd been robbed. He would not have minded her presence at all, he realized. It had been a long time since any woman had elicited such a reaction from him.

Wanda led them to one of the six tables occupying the opposite section of the diner and stopped at mid-point. "How's this?"

"Fine, thank you…" Before the woman could finish, the teenager had moved past her and dropped onto the red vinyl seat to the left of the table, patting her hands on the clean Formica top.

"No, Jazemara, the other side."

For a second the pretty young girl frowned and quickly slid out off the cushioned seat and sat in its opposite twin.

"Thank you," the woman sat in the spot vacated by her daughter and set down the carpetbag beside her.

She didn't want her back to the entrance. The thought came to Ravenwood unbidden. But he knew instinctively he was right. Who were they and what were they doing out at this late hour? The anxiousness he'd sensed from the woman and her desire to face the diner's only main door. What was she afraid of? Were they running away from someone? Or something?

After glancing at the torn cardboard menu, the alluring woman looked up at Wanda and asked for her advice. "My daughter and I are very hungry. We'd like something hot and filling …that will not take too long to prepare."

"Well, Jake still has some of tonight's meatloaf on the stove. He could cut you up some of that and put it on rye bread with mustard. Wouldn't take no time at all."

"Do you have any pie?" the girl asked, pulling off her cap and then her gloves.

"Sure thing, honey. We got apple and cherry. They're real yummy."

The daughter looked to her mother questioningly.

"Very well," she agreed, then gave Wanda their order for two meatloaf sandwiches to be followed by two slices of apple pie. "I'll have some coffee as well and you can bring my daughter some hot chocolate if you have any."

"I think I can rustle some up," the waitress said collecting the menus before she walked away and disappeared into the swinging door behind the counter. Her voice could be heard giving the cook their request.

Ravenwood took another drink of his coffee and mentally shrugged. He had to stop playing detective all the time. The way he had inspected the raven-haired woman and her child was silly. They were strangers of no concern to him and here he was letting his curiosity get the best of him; to include his unexpected feelings of arousal.

You are in danger, my son.

The thought that suddenly popped into his head was not his own. He recognized it immediately as a psychic warning from the Nameless One.

How? From where? He closed his eyes, attempting to receive his mentor's ethereal warning clearer.

The woman in black…beware!

There was a clinking sound followed by a rolling noise and then something small bumped into his left shoe. His eyes snapped opened, glanced down in time to see a round, silver medallion the size of a half-dollar fall over on the floor.

"I'm sorry, sir, it got away from me." The young girl had rushed over to retrieve what was obviously her coin.

He leaned over and picked it up and then held it up for her. "No need to apologize, young lady. Here is your runaway medallion." He noticed there was a German cross-embossed on its surface with words imprinted around the circumference. "Courage, loyalty and honor."

"You speak German?" The girl took the coin and smiled surprised by his ability to translate the inscription. Her eyes were infinite pools of deep blue-gray.

"Languages are a hobby of mine." He pointed to the coin. "That's a war medal, I believe. Awarded for exemplary courage in combat."

"It was my father's," she said. "Though I never met him. He died in the war. He was a famous flier. Mother says he was very brave."

"Then he has left you a proud legacy…."

"Mein Gott, your eyes!" the girl gasped realizing for the first time their strangeness. "They are not the same color!"

Ravenwood smiled. It was a reaction he was all too familiar with, having experienced it countless times in his life. "I have a medical condition known as hetrochromia, a difference of coloration in the irises. What are they now?"

The girl took a second to reply. "The left one is brown and the right one is a bright blue. What do you mean 'now.' Do they change?"

"Sometimes. Mine is a very rare case beyond the norm. My eyes change colors at random…without any warnings."

"Does it hurt?"

It was such a sweet and innocent question. Ravenwood was quickly becoming enamored with this girl. "No, not at all. In fact I'm never aware of when it happens…unless someone else points it out to me."

"Jazemara!" The girl's mother was noticeably annoyed. "Stop bothering the gentleman and return to your seat."

"Yes, mother." She started to comply with the order then suddenly leaned over and said in a conspiratorial whisper, "I'm Jazzy. Nice to meet you."

"I am Ravenwood and the pleasure is all mine, Jazzy."

Wanda was coming out of the swinging kitchen door just as the girl was returning to her seat to face her mother who merely looked at her with a stern expression. It spoke louder than any words of corrections.

"Here you go, ladies," Wanda said carefully placing the two plates down before the duo. "Two meatloaf sandwiches. Give me a second and I'll get your drinks."

As the friendly waitress started back around the corner, the front door opened and three men crowded into the diner. All of them were tall and brutish in appearance, wearing dark, soiled clothing and hats pulled down over their heads.

"Evening, gents," Wanda said stopping by the counter. "Just find a place to sit and I'll be right with you."

"That shall not be necessary," the closest man replied in a high-pitched voice. He looked at Jazzy and her mother. "We see what we've come for."

And with that, he reached out with his right hand and swiped it across Wanda's throat.

The second blood gushed from the woman's sliced throat, it splashed over her killer's face and he grinned, holding his hand to expose the inch long, razor sharp fingernails now coated in red. The mortally injured woman clutched at her severed throat trying to staunch the fountaining blood but it was useless.

She was dead long before she dropped to the floor.

Ravenwood came out of his booth clutching his silver tipped cane in his left hand.

One of the three intruders turned to him, tearing off his hat to expose his bald head and milk-white pallor. The fangs in his mouth accentuated his gaunt face. He was a vampire like his two companions.

"Really, a stick?" The monster charged him.

Ravenwood waited until the last possible moment and then reaching across his body, jerked the hidden rapier from its wooden scabbard and impaled the creature through the heart. The vampire was transfixed, his blood red eyes looking down at the steel in his chest. He snarled and grabbed for it with both hands.

"This will not stop me!"

He began to pull the blade from his body.

At the same time, across the diner, the other two vampires had turned their attention to the two women who were their real target.

"At long last, you are ours," the leader of the undead trio bragged as he approached their table slowly. His tongue flickered out over his fangs. "The master has waited long enough."

Just then the kitchen door banged open and Jake appeared holding a .38 revolver in his hands. Seeing Wanda's lifeless body on the floor, the mild-mannered cook was filled with righteous rage.

"You bastards!" He held the gun with both hands and fired point blank into the second vampire hitting him squarely in the chest with three rounds. The undead fiend was thrown off his feet into the coat rack by the door. He knocked over the wooden pole and steadied himself against the doorframe. Looking down at the holes in his coat, he shook his head and snarled like a vicious dog.

Before Jake could take a step back, the angry bloodsucker jumped him and together they disappeared through the kitchen portal. This was followed by the loud sounds of pots and pans clattering to the floor and then a piercing scream that was cut off suddenly.

At the same time Jazzy's mother sprang out of her seat grasping the porcelain plate on which her sandwiches had been delivered. Before the vampire could react, she whipped it around and smashed it into his face, her sandwich flying off in the opposite direction.

The strong plate shattered in her hands, shards cutting into the monster's dead flesh and breaking his nose. He growled and swiped at her with his long nails attempting to finish her as he had the helpless waitress. But the woman was faster and still holding the remaining piece of the smashed plate in her hand, she immediately drove it into the vampire's left eye with a powerful shove.

The monster bellowed and fell back from her.

Whereas Ravenwood was also backing up as he watched his opponent yank the rapier from his chest and toss it aside.

"Foolish mortal, I will make you suffer endlessly."

Ravenwood's right hand was behind his body groping for a particular object on the table. His fingers made contact and he clutched at the three-inch high glass container.

He whipped the saltshaker around, tore off the cap with his left hand and tossed its white granules into the vampire's descending mouth and face.

"You mean like this?"

The effect was instantaneous as the bits of salt bore into the vampire's flesh like tiny hot pokers; those in his mouth erupting into fiery spurts. His entire body was wracked with pain and began to shake violently as he attempted to wipe the burning pieces away and spit the others from his mouth. But it was too late and the fire inside his mouth seemed to flare brighter and burned his head from within. It burst into flames and he began spinning around wildly in the narrow aisle.

Ravenwood moved around the dancing, burning figure and bent to reclaim his rapier.

Meanwhile Jazzy's mother had taken a moment to turn her back on the vampire she had wounded to reach down and open her carry bag. She fumbled inside it and pulled out a foot-long gold crucifix that filled her hand and immediately held it out before her.

By now the crazed vampire had pulled the jagged piece of crockery from its ruined orb and was about to retaliate. At the sight of the cross, it screamed like a wild beast and put up its hands before its pale, gruesome face. It was in agony at the sight of the holy relic.

"Back you Satan spawned!" the brunette ordered, moving in closer.

Reluctantly the vampire shuffled back away from the offending cross.

"Jazzy, hurry!"

"Yes, mother."

The third undead by now had crumbled, burning away to ash before Ravenwood's startled eyes. So fast had his fiery consummation been that the white-hot flames hadn't lasted enough burn anything else in the confined space. Something the occult detective was grateful for.

He reached into his jacket and pulled his Luger from its under-the-arm holster and hurried to join the others in front of the door.

When the woman saw him over the shoulder of the vampire she was herding away from her and her daughter, she shook her head negatively. "Bullets cannot stop these....things."

Just then the kitchen door opened and the bloodied second vampire came rushing out.

Ravenwood twisted around and shot him in the head.

The monster stopped as it he had stuck a cement wall. His pink eyes rolled in their sockets and then he fell forward against the counter and was still.

The mysterious woman turned to Ravenwood who smiled, still holding tightly to his German made pistol. "I coat the bullets with Holy Water."

Then he shot the last vampire in the back of the head ending his threat forever.

"Who are you?" she asked puzzlement on her beautiful face. Her daughter remained hidden behind her.

"That's not important right now. Getting the two of you out here and to a safe place is. Will you trust me to do that?"

There was a moment's hesitation, then realizing she was still holding up her cross, she lowered her arm and said, "What other choice do we have? Lead on."

Ravenwood waited for her to retrieve her bag and then he opened the door and they stepped out into the night. He held his Luger at ready as he descended the three short steps to the pavement and pointed to the parked black convertible Alfa Romeo Spider Corsa in front of them. Its shiny surface reflected light spots from the nearby streetlamps. It was a small two-seater with the steering wheel on the right.

"But there's no room...?" the dark beauty said holding her daughter's arm with one hand and the heavy valise with the other.

Ravenwood dashed to the sleek sports car's rear and popped open the trunk. "Throw your bag in here. Jazzy will have to sit on your on your lap."

Just then there was a piercing howl and four dark clad shapes charged out of the alley across the street, their clawed hands reaching out; more vampires coming at them like a pack of ravenous wolves.

"HURRY!" Ravenwood stepped around the front of the Alpha Romeo and shot down two of the vampires in their tracks.

Before he could swing his aim to the third, the undead killer jumped over his head and landed on the Spider's rear cowling. Not seeing the older woman behind the upraised trunk, the monster sprang down onto Jazzy who barely had time to scream, "MOTHER!"

Transfixed by the sight of the high leaping vampire, Ravenwood had involuntarily taken his eyes off their fourth and last attacker. A second of distraction and suddenly he felt sharp nails digging into his arms as the monster was upon him, its fangs covered with drool, its awful fetid breath in his face. Holding his arms to his side in a superhuman grip, the hungry vampire lifted him off the ground. Its nails had penetrated the cloth of his coat and were digging deep into the flesh of his biceps.

He dropped the cane in his left hand but somehow willed himself to hold onto the Luger in his right, though there was no way he could ever bring it up in his current trapped state.

So be it.

Ravenwood twisted the automatic as best he could, imagining where the barrel was pointing and pulled the trigger.

His foe screamed and released him. It began jumping up and down on one foot, as it tried to hold up the foot he'd shot through with his tainted bullet. Dropping to the pavement, Ravenwood fired again at the creature, but because it was moving around so much his shot missed.

He remembered the two women and forgetting the wounded vampire, dashed around the small speedster in time to see Jazzy's mother come to her rescue.

The fiend atop the struggling teenager was pushing her hands down to clear an unobstructed path to her throat, its fangs exposed and eager to drink fresh blood. But it never got the chance as the enraged mother raced over and without hesitating kicked it in the side of the head with her pointed boot. The vampire fell over and onto its side. It tried to recover as Jazzy's mother stepped over her daughter to continue her assault on the unholy thing.

Unable to believe that a mere mortal woman was brave enough to confront it, the vampire sprang to its feet like a jumping jack, arms wide and ready. What it never saw coming was the ten-inch butcher's blade the woman suddenly withdrew from inside her cloak and the amazingly fast swing that cut off its head.

Dumbfounded by the woman's courage and lethalness, Ravenwood slammed the trunk lid closed and then went to help Jazzy get back on her feet.

"Your mother is a dangerous woman."

"You don't know the half of it," the girl said taking a deep breath.

"Save it for later." Ravenwood watched the woman kick the vampire's head down the sidewalk and approved. "Come on! Get in the car before any more of them show up!"

He put away his Luger, climbed into the car and kicked over the engine, setting his cane down beside him. As the racing engine roared to life, the woman ran around the front of the Spider, pulled open the door and fell back into the passenger seat while motioning her daughter to follow her.

At the same time the one-legged, hoping Vampire had stopped his crazy dance and was started to limp towards them.

The second Jazzy fell back onto her mother's lap, Ravenwood popped the clutch, pressed down on the gas pedal and the black Spider shot away down the road; the passenger door slamming shut with the forward motion.

Behind them the crippled vampire raised its arms toward the night sky and cried out in rage.

—)|(—

"Your mother is a dangerous woman."

Baron Henri Savigne detested America with its New World opulence and upstart haughty airs as if it, by its very youth as a nation, was somehow better than the old world civilizations from which it had sprung. This condescending air of its people wherever he and his entourage traveled was offensive and continually fed his righteous indignation. Having to endure Americans and their uncivilized mannerism was perhaps the greatest challenge he had faced in well over three hundred years of existence; both as a human and now as one of the nosferatu.

In fact, the only thing of worth in the whole of this decadent metropolis they called New York was its abundance of fresh, wholesome blood; free for the taking.

As a Lord of the Imperial Vampire Court, he had smelled the ripe life-giving plasma coursing through the veins of the mindless human cattle all around him. How he yearned to unleash his bestial nature and feed freely on them as was his right. But the Court had made it quite clear that no such rampant blood shedding would be permitted during this hunt. Their mission was focused on one single objective, find the woman and her special child; capture them and return them to Paris. There they would be delivered to the Royal Court.

Looking about the dingy warehouse he had chosen as their base of operation, the ancient vampire could hear tramp steamers moving up and down the waterways of the Hudson River, their mournful whistles crying out in the night. At his feet, one of the two prostitutes he had fed on minutes earlier began to stir. Apparently he had not completely drained painted hussy as he had her companion. Baron Savigne signaled one of his minions, the burly Berleze, to come forth.

There was twelve of his undead troop, of both genders, scattered about the large, dank and cold warehouse. He commanded twice as many; the others were out scouring the night streets in search of their prey. He rotated them in shifts worried that too many on the loose simultaneously would invariably expose their presence and lead to disaster. He would not fail his superiors. Success could easily mean a place on the court for him when the time was right.

"Yes, my lord?" Berleze had been a miller from Belgium and somewhat dimwitted before having been turned. It annoyed the vampire leader to have to deal with him, but the brutish being's immense strength had increased ten-fold upon becoming one of the undead and thus he was a rare asset to the baron. Berleze's primary task was the protection of his master.

"Get rid of them," the baron commanded wiping his blood stained lips and chin with a silk handkerchief. "But be sure to take their off heads before you dispose of them.

"Do you understand?"

"Yes, master," the pale giant smiled grotesquely. "You do not want them to rise again."

"Indeed. The last thing we need is free agents running around attacking people and thus alerting the authorities to our presence in their midst."

Berleze reached down and picked up the groaning whore by the back of the neck. He broke it with a snap and then hoisted the body over his right shoulder. Effortlessly he picked up the remaining dead woman and set her on his left side before walking off towards the building's main double doors.

Another of the vampires, seeing Berleze marching by with his burden, raced over and pulled back one side of the portal only to jump back in surprise as a figure suddenly appeared from the dark outside.

"Gustof!" the would-be doorman mouthed, recognizing one of the six that had been dispatched earlier that evening.

Without acknowledging his fellow bloodsucker, Gustof pushed past him and moving with a very noticeable limp skirted around the big Berleze. By now all the lifeless eyes in the room were on the crippled vampire as he painfully marched up to his master where he came to a halt and bowed his head.

Baron Savigne, on his raised dais made from wooden pallets, looked down upon the one called Gustof. "Where are the others? And why are you limping?"

"We found them!" Gustof blurted, ignoring the questions put to them. "In a cheap diner near the theater district."

Savigne sat up straighter and leaned forward. "What? Are you sure?"

"Yes, my lord, it was them; the woman and her daughter. Their scent was unmistakable."

"Then where are they?" The vampire liege spread out his hands. "Why are they not here bound before me? And where are your cohorts. Tell me they have the bitch and her whelp and are now in the process of bringing them here."

At this Gustof seemed to shudder slightly. His pinkish eyes looked about furtively as all the others in the room had moved closer and were now encircling him, all as eager as their master to hear his words. Only the massive Berleze was absent, having simply continued on with his assignment as he was ordered. Even the sudden appearance of Gustof had not aroused the slightest iota of curiosity in the big vampire's mind. He only lived to obey his master.

"She escaped us…"

"WHAT!" The baron stood, anger shaping his face.

"….with the help of a stranger." Gustof clutched his hands together in front of his chest as if in prayer, shrinking in upon himself. "He had weapons…the bullets from his gun somehow manage to …to…"

"To what? Speak up you sniveling cur."

"They hurt …they could harm us…and did. With his help, they slew the others…all of them. Never to rise again."

There was a hushed murmur as the gathered vampires whispered amongst themselves at this incredible revelation.

"How is that even possible?' Baron Savigne stepped off his raised platform and stood before his frightened subject. "This stranger slew our brethren, left you wounded and then escaped with the countess and her child."

"Yes, my lord. That is what happened."

The vampire lord felt his anger rising and realized the folly of such a reaction. He could not afford the luxury of an uncontrollable rage.

Walking around the still worrisome Gustof, he motioned to several of the others. "Very, well, Gustof, I will accept your account, as ludicrous as it sounds. It only makes our task all the more difficult.

"We must learn the identity of this interloper and deal with him. But first I wish to examine these bullets with which he decimated six of my fellows."

At that the four vampires he had chosen stepped forward and took hold of Gustof and pulled him onto his back on the rough cement floor. He tried to fight them off, but it was useless.

"Remove his shoe." The baron raised his right hand the fingernails began to swell outward until they looked like talons. "Now, hold him steady while I retrieve this so-called…magic bullet."

⟶⟍⟋⟵

It only took Ravenwood twenty minutes to drive to his apartment penthouse in the richest part of Manhattan. Going up the private elevator to his top floor suite, he was mildly amused at the young lift operator's reaction to his two guests. Sammy Edwards had been employed at the hotel for several years and had seen many strange types going up to Ravenwood's sanctum, but none as exotically beautiful as the dark haired woman or her cap-wearing teenage daughter.

They exited onto the fifth floor and entered a short hallway that led directly to the main entrance to his home. Ravenwood was carrying the woman's carpetbag in his free hand, his walking cane with the other.

"There are no other tenants?" asked the woman. She had remained stoically silence during the speedy ride from the diner.

"No," Ravenwood replied, slipping his key into the front door and opening it. "The entire floor is mine."

"And you live alone," she guessed walking past him as he swept his arm to invite the ladies into a lighted foyer.

"Hardly," he said, closing the door and then pressing an intercom button on the wall. "Sterling, we have guest. Meet us in my office."

There was a crackle from the speaker mesh and then a British voice was heard. "Yes, sir, at once."

With that, Ravenwood led the two women down a short corridor and into a large, ornately decorated room filled with bookshelves along the left and back walls. A massive wooden desk was set directly opposite the entrance and to their immediate right were fancy French doors covered with linen drapes. They opened onto a balcony with a spectacular view of the downtown. A fancy oriental rug covered the majority of the hardwood floor and to either side of it was a plush-looking sofa. Two leather clad chairs, both a russet brown faced the desk itself.

Ravenwood flicked the light switch and two standing lamps behind the sofas lighted the room. The room had an old-world feel to it and Jazzy was immediately taken with its atmosphere, especially the look of the rare tomes that filled the floor to ceiling bookshelves.

"Oh, mother, look," she exclaimed, moving along the wall, her finger touching the worn spines. "They are all about philosophy and magic."

Once again, Jazzy's mother turned her inquisitive green eyes to their host and repeated her earlier question. "Just exactly who are you and why are you armed as you are?"

"My name is Ravenwood, madam," he bowed slightly. "And I'm an investigator of the occult; thus my unusual weaponry. This was not my first encounter with the undead."

"Really." The woman bit her lower lip reflecting on his answer.

Just then Sterling, the tall, gray-haired butler, appeared behind them wearing a stylish robe over his black pajamas and wearing slippers. "Good evening, sir. Ladies."

"Ah, Sterling, there you are." Ravenwood smiled. "Please fix the guest bedroom, our guests will be spending the night."

"Very well sir. If the ladies wish, I can relieve them of their coats and hats."

Jazzy and her mother began removing their outer garments, relieved to be doing so while Ravenwood handed Sterling the heavy bag. "And after you've done, be so kind as to prepare a small repast for them. I know they have not dined this evening and must both be famished."

"Oh, no," the brunette said handing her hooded cloak to the waiting servant. Beneath she wore a simple, yellow cotton dress with short sleeves. "We don't want to put you to any more trouble."

"No trouble at all, Madam," the long faced Sterling declared. "It will only take me a few minutes to prepare a platter of cold meats and cheeses."

"That sounds great," Jazzy said holding her own coat and hat in her arms. "I'm really hungry, mother."

"Very well then. But why don't you accompany Mr. Sterling. He seems to have his hands full."

"Alright," the girl beamed, looking up at the stiff-necked Brit. "Hi, I'm Jazzy. Do have any peanut butter?"

Sterling crunched his face for a second before responding, "I do believe there is such an item in the food pantry. Come along, Miss ...ah...Jazzy. This way."

Ravenwood closed the door after them and invited Jazzy's mother to sit. She chose the nearest sofa as he went around his desk where he removed his jacket and draped it over the back of the swivel chair. He unfastened his shoulder holster with his Luger pistol and set it on the table next to a crystal decanter set.

"Would you join me in a brandy while we wait for Sterling to prepare your room?"

The woman arched her back and stretched her arms up over her head. "A brandy would be wonderful, Mr. Ravenwood. I confess, my nerves are rather frayed by what just happened."

As Ravenwood reached for the glass bottle, he heard the Nameless One's voice in his mind.

You brought her here! Into our sanctuary!

What was I supposed to do? Leave her and the child on the streets at the mercy of their foes?

There is an old spirit that surrounds her, my son. You must proceed with great care. This is like no other woman you have ever met.

Accepting his mentor's silent warning, the occult detective poured the ruby red liqueur into two small glasses. "From the conversation I overheard, you and Jazzy have been running from these creatures. Is that true?"

"It is," she sighed, dropping her arms and folding them under her bosom. "Ours is not a simple story."

He came over, handed her a glass and sat down at the other end of the settee. They both took a sip of the fiery elixir. Once more her radiant beauty was almost overpowering. Her alluring green eyes bore into him like those of a stalking tiger. "I assumed as much, madam....ah....perhaps we should start with your name."

"Dracula, sir. I am the Countess Marya Dracula, daughter of Count Vlad Dracula the Second of Wallachia. The one history has come to know as Vlad the Impaler."

—/|\—

In his years as an occult detective, Ravenwood had heard many strange tales but none was as fantastic as that related to him by the mysterious dark haired beauty who now faced him.

"In the year 1412, hordes of Turks swept across the mid-eastern Romania's bent on the total conquest of the Christian Empire. My father, a knight in the Order of St. George, watched his armies slaughtered in battle after battle. The invading barbarians butchered the women folk of our homeland lamented in agony as fathers, sons, husbands and lovers and it appeared all was lost.

"Facing total defeat, seeing his people suffering, my father came to believe that God had abandoned him. In anger he lashed out at the church itself, publicly cursing the very cross he had once sworn to defend.

"During a particularly violent storm, my father walked across the last battlefield covered with the bodies of his men. In a passionate rage, he raised his gloved fists to the dark skies and there offered his allegiance to Satan and all his dark principalities if it would bring him victory and save his beloved Transylvania."

Marya took another sip of her brandy before continuing. "This part I'm afraid is hearsay, told to me by my father years later."

Ravenwood nodded. "Understood. Please continue."

"Apparently Lucifer heard my father's dire request for upon uttering it he was struck by lightning and hurled many yards into a lone standing tree. That he was not instantly killed was a sign that his petition had been granted. Rising to his feet, his armor smoking, Vlad Dracula was no longer human; he had become a vampire; one of the undead.

"What followed next is well documented in the history of our lands. Leading his remaining forces with his new, unholy powers, he became a true monster of death and destruction. When the Mongols discovered he could not be killed, they fled before him and Transylvania was saved.

"Racing to rejoin his family, my poor father was to learn there was yet another price to be paid for his pact with the devil. Before fleeing, a company of Mongols had attacked our castle and savagely butchered everyone within its walls.

"My mother and brothers were tortured and slain...all before my eyes..."

Tears began to slip down Marya's cheeks as she tried shaking loose the awful memories now resurfacing inside her. Ravenwood moved closer and put his hand over hers.

"How foolish of me," she apologized. "Tears are not something I easily shed, Mr. Ravenwood."

"Just Ravenwood, please. I take it you were not spared your own tribulations."

"That is putting it mildly. By the time my father and his men reached the castle, it was in ruins. And as you surmised, I too had been a victim of the Mongol's animal lust for vengeance and lay twisted and broken at the age of twelve before my father's tortured gaze. Heartbroken, he knelt and cradled me in his arms unwilling to lose me, the last of his children and so he did the only thing he could to save me; he gave me the kiss of the vampire.

"Yes, Ravenwood, I too would rise again and thus began our journey together through time as the last of the Draculas. The invasion quelled, the people of the surrounding villages pledged themselves to us in gratitude for what my father had done. They vowed to serve us faithfully as long as we continued to walk the earth.

"For the next four hundred years, we existed in the seclusion of our ancestral home, feeding off the blood of the living. I am sorry if this repulses you."

Both of them drained their glasses and Ravenwood took her empty glass. "I'll wait until I've heard the entire tale before judging you, countess."

"Marya, please. The old ways are ghosts in this new modern age."

"You say you were turned at the age of twelve," Ravenwood pointed out as he stood and brought the glasses back to his desk. "It is obvious that even as a vampire, you continued to mature."

"Yes, I did. Somewhere in my twenty-fifth year I ceased aging completely. And as long as I continued to feed, maintained my youth and supernatural vigor."

Ravenwood returned to the sofa and sitting, smiled awkwardly. "And still it is obvious you have aged still further."

Marya Dracula brought her left hand up to her black hair with its few strands of gray and returned his smile. "You are gallant, sir. Yes, at present I am ….well, let us say, I am now aging as any other woman does."

This brought a puzzled expression to his face and Marya went on with her story.

"Eventually my father could no longer withstand our confinement and dared to begin traveling abroad until he found himself in Great Britain where he met a young lady who bore a striking resemblance to my mother. Blinded by her appearance, he became reckless and his true nature was revealed. Thus he was trapped and finally put to death forever.

"You can well imagine my sorrow when I learned of his fate. For the first time since all these horrific events had begun; I was truly alone in the world. Back then, I had no inkling there were others such as I; something I would only discover much later to my misfortune. In the meanwhile, I resigned myself to my solitary existence. My only social interaction was with those villagers who continued to fill the ranks of the castle's staff from one generation to the next. They, and the wretched victims they would procure for me in their devotion to their ages old pledge.

"Thus my cursed existence until the eve of the Great War when it seemed the whole world had gone crazy. Then a chance meeting on the grounds of our estate began a chain of events that would alter my future and prove to be the salvation of my soul. I met a young German lad named Manfred von Richthofen."

━╱╲━

"The bloody Red Baron was your father!" Sterling almost dropped the pitcher of milk in his hands at Jazzy's proclamation of her lineage. They were in the large, spotlessly clean kitchen. She was seated at the table spreading huge gobs of peanut butter on slices of French bread while Ravenwood's butler was about to pour her a glass of milk before he cut up cheese and cold meats for her mother and his employer.

"Hmm…hmmm," she mumbled chewing on the delicious spread.

"Mother said they met just before the war started and she fell in love with him the second she met him. Enough so that she traveled the Berlin years later to find him again."

Sterling poured the milk while his thoughts went back in time. "Amazing, truly amazing. You see, I was a pilot myself, Miss Jazzy, in the Royal Air Force. I flew in many aerial duels over the ravaged landscapes of France and Germany."

"You mean dogfights." She swallowed a mouthful while reaching for the cold white milk. She took a long drink. Wiping her mouth with a napkin, she asked, "Did you ever see my father? Mother says his Fokker was painted a very bright red."

"Indeed it was," Sterling confirmed. "But I had the good fortune to never see it personally. Had I done so, I might not be here today. Your father was one of the greatest aces to ever take to the skies.

"I remember when we received word that he had been shot down..." Sterling realized the words coming from his mouth and looked at the bright-eyed young girl with apprehension. "Oh...forgive me..."

"It's okay, really." Jazzy dug into the jar of peanut butter with the butter knife he had given her. "I never really knew him. He died before I was even born." She smeared the brown goop on another slice of bread. "To me he's just a story."

Sterling went to the icebox to fetch the cheese and salami roll. "Still, you should be proud of your heritage, Miss Jazzy. He was truly a remarkable, brave man."

"I suppose." She started nibbling on her treat. "Still, the greatest thing he really did was stop mother from being a vampire."

Sterling dropped the block of cheese.

—✈—

"You can imagine my insane rage upon learning of Manny's death," Marya continued her incredible tale. "Hell hath no fury as woman scorned, I believe is how the Bard put it."

"But by then you were pregnant with Jazzy?"

"I was...but I didn't know it yet. I was filled with an all-consuming hatred for the Allied fliers who had taken my love from me. Manfred had wiped out five hundred years of loneliness with his caresses and then, in a cruel twist of fate, he was taken from me.

"The weeks following his death were a blur. I used all of my dark powers to lay waste to Allied squadrons and commanded thousands of rats to swarm over their airdromes. My need for revenge blinded me to all else.

"And then, one morning, returning to the safety of Castle Dracula before the sun's rise, I collapsed in excruciating pain before my servant, Irena; an old woman who had been with me for many years. I vomited blood, so much....it just spewed out of me as if my body could not longer accept it."

"Something that had never happened before." Ravenwood could sense the weariness in Marya and that she was coming to climax of her story.

"Of course not. I was a vampire. Human blood was what sustained me. Why should I now suddenly be unable to digest it? Of course it was wise Irena who guessed the answer."

"You were pregnant with Jazzy."

"Yes, as impossible as that was for me to believe. How could something alive take seed in something foul and undead such as I?

"Irena argued that it was Manfred's true love that had brought about this miracle and if in fact I could no longer drink the blood of others, then it meant the curse of my vampirism had been lifted; that I was once again mortal.

"But how could I be certain? How could I be absolutely sure I was no longer one of the undead, that the Almighty in his infinite mercy had forgiven me? Of course the answer was simple enough. All I had to do was leave the darkness interior of the castle and venture forth into the sunlight of the new day exposing myself to a sun I had not beheld in over five hundred years."

At this point Marya took a deep breath and exhaled it slowly.

"I take it you survived the test."

She looked at him and nodded. "It is a moment I shall never forget, Ravenwood, as long as I have left in this world. To walk out on that parapet overlooking our vast estate and feel the warm rays of the sun bathe my flesh in a euphoric baptism of redemption.

"I fell to my knees, clasped my hands together in prayer and gave thanks to a truly loving God who does forgive beyond our imagination.

"The rest all happened swiftly enough. I had the castle boarded up and left it to begin my...*our* new life. I traveled to Belgium and there gave birth to Jazemara and remained there for several years. Keep in mind, our family's wealth was hidden away in banks across Europe and my daughter and I wanted for nothing.

"Those were glorious, happy years. As Jazemara grew...so did I, like any normal woman should. But I was no longer afraid of the process or the fact that one day I too would pass from this reality into the next. Having been granted so powerful a miracle, I was truly humbled and daily appreciative of the truest treasure this world has to offer, love."

Marya paused then as if reliving every memory just as she had related them. In the quiet between them Ravenwood could not help but believe her sincerity. As outrageous as the tale appeared, he believed every word of it.

As you should, my son. The Nameless One's mental confirmation was tremendously assuring. Ravenwood had been well aware his old mentor had been listening to the woman's account through his eyes. Something he was skilled at doing.

Everything she has said is the truth. But as before, she and the girl are still in grave danger and it will be your decision as to whether to send them or their way or become involved with their plight.

But father, I could only act as you've taught me. In his mind he saw the Nameless One's tiny smile. He'd given him the right answer.

"Alright, Marya," he broke the mental contact. "Who are these vampires chasing you and Jazzy?"

Before Dracula's daughter could answer that question, Sterling reappeared pushing a cart on which was a silver platter filled with cheeses and meat and a carafe of coffee surrounded by porcelain cups. Jazzy waltzed in behind him holding a large mug of hot cocoa.

Sterling brought the wheeled cart to the center of the room, put his arms behind his back and asked, "Will this do, sir?"

⸙

As the amiable Sterling set about feeding his employer and his guests, the Nameless One sat cross-legged on his padded floor mat in his small, square room. Situated in the exact center of the penthouse, it was the only room without any windows and the old man preferred it as such. The only furniture in the room was a wooden bed against one wall and a tiny wooden altar against the back wall opposite the single door. On this rested an ivory sculptured statue of the Buddha. On either side of the figure were two scented candles that filled the tiny room with a pleasant, woodsy smell. The room was equipped with electricity and an overhead light was affixed to the ceiling but the Nameless One never used it, the noise of the speeding electrons disturbed his meditation.

His old mentor had been listening to the woman's account through his eyes.

Now, seated on the floor before the white Buddha, he began to slow his breathing and enter into a deep meditative state. He was a small figure, his aged body virtually devoid of any excess fat, his thin limbs tough, his weathered skin tanned almost bronze. He wore his pale white hair shoulder length and a thin gossamer-like beard fell to his chest. He was dressed in gray cotton pants and a matching button-less tunic.

As he began humming the holy Tibetan mantras he had been taught as a child, he unconsciously ran his bony fingers through his beard, a habit he had developed to soothe his always-curious mind and allow him to draw deep within his own soul. His eyes closed welcoming the dark warmth of the universe around him and he continued to hum, his breathing lessening with each rhythmic beat of his powerful heart. Deeper he fell into his own being until a light appeared before him. He sent his true astral body after it.

Just like that he was floating in the air before his physical body; an experience he had undergone more times than he could remember. He prepared to fly out and find those agents of evil that threatened his adoptive son.

His invisible specter glided through the walls of his room, down the corridor and into Ravenwood's office where the others were gathered. The woman with the black hair was conversing while pausing every few minutes to partake of the nourishment the butler had delivered. Though old beyond reckoning, the Nameless One could still appreciate true beauty when he beheld it and at seeing Marya Dracula he understood why his American son was smitten with her. At the same time the daughter's aura was charged with a golden energy and the Nameless One saw in her a powerful spirit capable of much potential if she were protected and kept from the clutches of those who hunted them.

Father? Ravenwood had sensed his astral presence but didn't let on to the others, continuing to be an attentive host while aware of his nearness.

I go to find the evil ones and their nest. Remain vigilant. When I return, I will call you and the countess to my room.

As you wish, Old One.

And with that the one time Tibetan monk floated up through the ceiling, through the buildings roof and out into the skies over Manhattan.

For any lesser spirit, the task before him would have been hopeless. Manhattan was the home to millions, each emanating a spiritual light. A lesser Yogi would have been unable to discern individual souls amidst this mighty assemblage, their *chis* merging together in a swirling whirlpool of humanity. But Tibetan monks who were masters of astral projection had taught the Nameless One and his ability to differentiate amongst the multitude below him was his true power.

The sky over the city was a blue-black canvas. In the distance, beyond the harbor were small flashes of lightning and he could feel the moisture in the molecules around him. A storm was coming and with it rain. As he flew over the buildings and streets below, the Nameless One made no effort to guide his essence in any particular direction. All the while his soul continued to receive impressions from the ether, signals from the populace beneath him. Thoughts of decency, charity, love as well as those of cruelty, sadism and pure selfishness. All washed through him as he floated freely through the cloudless heavens.

He was looking down at the Hudson River when the odorous wave of occult bestiality assaulted him. So strong was its essence he was nearly shaken from his self-induced trance and hurled back into his physical shell; still at rest back in his room. Girthing his mental shield, the Nameless One followed the evil essence downward to its source and he found himself hovering above a squat, broken down warehouse abutting the piers of an abandoned dock site. As he descended lower to the roof the stench of the undead permeated him completely.

This was it; the secret enclave of the foreign vampires. No sooner had that thought arisen in his consciousness then he saw several scurrying figures appear from the alley beside the warehouse. Moving more like animals than people, the Nameless One watched the vampires hurry to the warehouse's front entrance and slip inside. He could make out the street number over the sliding doors.

It was enough. To go any further might alert the foul things as their own supernatural abilities were many. No, he had achieved his goal. Lifting his arms wide, the Nameless One rose into the air as thunder rolled in from the shores of New Jersey.

He opened his eyes....and was back in his room.

—⟩⟨—

"When Jazemara was six, we left Belgium for Paris," Marya Dracula related as she put down her empty coffee cup. "I wanted her to have a broad education; to be familiar with various world cultures and such. Paris was such a cosmopolitan atmosphere."

Ravenwood nodded as Jazzy made a face to let her mother know for the millionth time how much she did not like her own name. It was so old fashioned. Meanwhile, Sterling sat on the opposite sofa, awaiting any further instructions. His hastily put-together repast has been well picked over by their lovely guest and now Marya was finishing the story of their ordeal.

"It truly is a wonderfully city," Ravenwood concurred. "I was happy to learn it had not suffered any great damage from the war."

"Oh, no, it is very much the center of the new bohemian movement," Marya continued. "What with artists and poets from around Europe gathering there to create a brand renaissance." She sighed. "The very thing to attract those who dwell in the shadows.

"You see, it was there that we were approached by agents of the Imperial Vampire Court. Although I had vague memories of my father having mentioned we were not the only ones of our kind, his words had long since faded from my thoughts and in my naiveté at being cured, I foolishly ignored the possibilities that other such....creatures still walked amongst the dark alleys of world.

"You can imagine my surprise when I was visited one night by two gentlemen in fancy clothing identifying themselves as vampires sent by this so-called Court to contact me in regards to Jazemara's lineage and her supposed destiny."

"How so?" Ravenwood started to get up, his own cup empty. Sterling, ever watchful, jumped to his feet, took the mug and refilled it without spilling a drop.

"Thank you, Sterling." The butler nodded and returned to his place on the long sofa.

"They want me to be their new Queen of the Vampires," Jazzy blurted out, seeing the pause in her mother's explanation. "All because I'm Dracula's granddaughter."

"Jazemara, please do not interrupt me."

"Sorry. But it's true."

"Yes, my dear. That was the purpose of their visit." Marya looked at Ravenwood, her green eyes imploring him to understand her fears. "Somehow this group of elite vampires had learned of Jazemara's birth and saw it as some kind of a sign—that she should become their queen."

"But she isn't even a vampire?" Sterling said caught up in the story. "Ah... is she?"

He turned his gaze to Jazzy who immediately stuck out her tongue at him.

"Of course not, Mr. Sterling. Jazemara was conceived in true, pure love. A love so powerful it cleansed my own soul and she has never once exhibited the slightest hint of that foul tainting."

"Then for her to assume this role she would have to be turned," Ravenwood finished for Marya.

"Something that will never happen as long as I live," Marya's words were hard edged. "Knowing how precarious our position was, in a strange city with no real allies, I lied and told them their proposal was something I needed time to consider...that maybe, instead of Jazemara, I could once again join their ranks and assume that role.

"My words seemed to placate them and they departed saying they would return within a week for my answer. I realized our only recourse was to leave Paris and that very night I packed what few belongings we had and we fled."

"Where did you go?"

"England. It was but a short journey across the channel and once there, we took up residency in a small hamlet on the coast of Wales far from the major populace centers such as London or Manchester. I prayed we had successfully eluded them and for the next few years we did. But they are relentless, if nothing else, and eventually tracked us down. Once again we fled. This time across the ocean to Canada where we lived until a few months ago."

"Where they found you again." Ravenwood found the vampires' obsession formidable indeed. If they were willing to chase half way around the world for Marya and her daughter, what could possibly stop them?

"Yes. They attacked us one evening as I was picking her up from a school dance. I was just barely able to fend them off long enough for us to reach the train station and book passage south. That was three days ago, Ravenwood. We haven't stopped running since."

"Then," said a very soft voice, "perhaps it is time you did so, dear lady."

All eyes turned to the open doorway where the old man in the gray clothing stood, his arms folded casually behind his back. Sterling nearly fell off the sofa, so rare were the times when the Nameless One ventured outside his room.

Ravenwood had almost the same reaction, rising to his feet and greeting his revered mentor. "Father. Let me introduce you to our guests; the Countess Marya Dracula and her daughter, Jazemara."

The Nameless One bowed slightly and then grinned at the teenage girl. "I trust your mother will forgive me," he said. "But I too like Jazzy much better."

Having put them at ease, the Nameless One turned to the butler. "It has been a long night. Could I possibly trouble you for a cup of herbal tea?"

"I suppose I can find something in the pantry." Sterling rose with a huff and exited the room.

Marya, sensing his ire, turned to Ravenwood who merely shrugged. "Cats and dogs, they are like this all the time."

"My intention was not to annoy your servant, my son. But rather, I believe I have the answer to the countess' situation. One that will effectively end the threat of the Vampire Court to her and Jazzy forever."

"How could you do that?" Marya asked surprised by the old man's claim.

"Well, in two ways, dear lady. The first is to effectively eliminate the present threat to you here in this place."

"And the second?"

"To deliver you and Mistress Jazzy to a place no evil can ever find you again."

—⁊∣↖—

Inspector Horatio Stagg marched up and down the sidewalk in front of the abandoned waterfront warehouse like a frustrated marionette on strings. He was a short, chunky man with deep set eyes and reminded people of a human bulldog with his brown derby and rumpled corduroy suit of the same color. His officers respected him as a by-the-book honest cop who never shirked his duties. Inspector Stagg would never ask any of them to do anything he would not do himself.

Which was why twelve of them, in their dark blue uniforms, were gathered together in front of four parked radio cars awaiting his orders. Waiting to learn why they had been ordered to this river dockside as a glaring yellow sunrise splashed across the skies behind them. There was a predawn chill in the air signifying that autumn wasn't too far off. All around them were stevedores arriving for work to unload the giant ships waiting at anchor to divest themselves of their various cargoes.

Stagg and his men had arrived fifteen minutes earlier as directed by Ravenwood. Although the inspector was a skeptic and didn't believe in all the supernatural mumbo-jumbo that was Ravenwood's stock and trade, he couldn't deny the man had helped him on several occasions when certain cases involved bizarre, unexplained phenomena. In his cop's heart, he knew it was all a con, tricks to pull the wool over gullible civilians. But not him, no sirree. Horatio Stagg knew better.

Which only infuriated him more. Here he was with his men wasting time all because of a midnight phone call from Ravenwood requesting his help. When Stagg had asked for specifics, the eccentric investigator had replied vaguely about some nest of monsters threatening the city. Monsters! Really!

Stagg started to reach into his jacket pocket to grab a handful of roasted peanuts from the paper bag he always carried when the sound of a sports car turned his attention to the corner. Ravenwood's sleek black Alfa Romeo Spider Corsa appeared and speeded to where the police vehicles were parked. It came to a smooth stop and Stagg hurried over as the engine died and Ravenwood, looking tired, climbed out. At the same time a tall, striking woman emerged from the passenger side wearing a hooded cloak. Giving her a cursory glimpse, the veteran cop greeted the Stepson of Mystery in his usual manner.

"Alright, fancy pants, what the hell is going on that necessitated you dragging me and my men out here at the bloody crack of dawn?"

"Good morning to you as well, Inspector," Ravenwood maintained a straight face as he turned and walked to the rear of his automobile. "I am most grateful for your willingness to meet us here. Allow me to open the trunk and I'll explain what we are all doing here."

As Ravenwood unlocked the boot and raised the cover, Marya came to stand by his side. In the trunk was a huge canvas bag, which the occult detective opened wide for Stagg to inspect.

In it were dozens of wooden stakes, each a foot long, four heavy mallets, some machetes and several silver flasks filled with Holy Water.

"What the hell is all this for?" Stagg asked picking up one of the big mallets and several stakes. "You hunting vampires now?"

Despite himself, Ravenwood smiled. "Inspector Stagg, you never fail to astound me with your honed deductive skills. That is exactly what we are here for." He moved around the inspector and pointed to the warehouse. "We will find them hidden inside. Most likely resting in their coffins now that the sun has risen. It is the time they are the most vulnerable."

Stagg stood with his mouth agape. By now several of his men had come closer and heard Ravenwood's declaration. All their eyes were on their leader.

Stagg blinked and then started to laugh, tossing the mallet and stakes back into the trunk. "Jesus, Mary, Joseph, Ravenwood, you've finally gone completely bonkers. Vampires!! God…if that ain't the funniest thing…"

Marya stepped up behind the ranting copper and grabbed him by the back of the neck. With one hand she lifted him off his feet. He yelled in surprise, his feet kicking in the air, his eyes frantically trying to look back at who it was holding him so easily.

"You think vampires are amusing?" Marya snarled. "I assure you, sir, they are not. They are real predators who will inflict great harm unless you aid us in destroying them here and now."

"Geezus…lady…put me down!"

Marya complied none too gently. Stagg stumbled and put out a hand to steady himself. Then, catching his breath, spun around to face the countess. "How the hell did you do that?"

"I was once a vampire. The strength it took to pick you up just now is but a small example of the powers I once possessed. Powers wielded by all the foul things hiding in that building at this very moment.

"Vampires are real, inspector. Ignore that and the horrors that will follow will be on your head."

Horatio Stagg swallowed hard. As much as he was angry for being publicly humiliated in front of his men, the grim look in Marya's eyes gave him pause. *What if she and Ravenwood were telling the truth? A vampire scourge on Manhattan!* A sick look came over his face. What other choice did he have? If Ravenwood was crazy, they'd break into the warehouse, find it empty and then he could lock him up, and the crazy strong dame, for any number of minor misdemeanors. On the other hand if they were legit…

"Alright," he muttered, turning back to Ravenwood. "But if all this is some kind of hoax, I'll lock you away so fast, you won't know what hit you."

"Fair enough, Inspector." Ravenwood nodded towards the trunk. "Can we proceed now?"

Stagg pointed to two of the nearest policemen. "Carter and Monroe, you two grab that duffel bag inside the trunk and follow us. The rest of you draw your guns and be ready for anything." At that the boys in blue unholstered their revolvers except for the two men assigned to carry the heavy canvas bag.

Seeing this, Ravenwood and Marya started up the cement steps leading to the platform and the twin sliding doors that opened into the warehouse. Stagg was immediately behind them, his own .38 clutched in his right hand.

There was no lock of any kind on either door and the veteran detective pushed past Ravenwood, grabbed a wooden handle and pulled it sideways. It made very little noise as it slid away on steel rollers leaving them facing the darkened interior.

The harsh light of the new day fell over their shoulders, its presence a comforting element as they eyed the stygian blackness that awaited them inside the massive, empty building.

Not one to hesitate, Inspector Horatio Stagg marched forward into what appeared to be a wide-open space. The cement floor was covered with a thick layer of dust now being kicked up by his footfalls. There was a dim light from high over head and he looked up to see long, tall windows that had been covered by a thick green paint, still they could not completely blot out the outdoor light.

Ravenwood and Marya flanked him to either side, both moving just cautiously as their eyes gradually adjusted to the gloomy interior. The place reminded Stagg of an empty church being so vast and spread out. He would not have minded a few candles here and there. His shoes stepped on something brittle and he stopped to look down. Reaching into his coat pocket he pulled out a wooden match and lit it by scratching it with his thumbnail. Immediately the robust flame illuminated his torso.

"What?" Ravenwood turned to him.

"I'm stepping on something weird." Stagg bent over slightly with the burning match and revealed the carcasses of dozens of dead rats and mice. "Sweet Jesus! What the hell?"

"Seems our friends were snacking," Ravenwood suggested wryly.

Before the light burned out, one of the uniformed men behind them called out. "Over there, up ahead. Are those crates?"

The group moved forward until the shapes became familiar pieces of furniture; a few desks covered with paper litter and a half dozen wooden chairs fallen over. Stagg lit another match and was pleasantly surprised to find several candles scattered amidst the clutter on the desktops. He picked one up and hurriedly lit the wick tip before his match went out.

"Some of you guys light those other candles," he directed.

Soon four candles were aglow and the visible area around them began to widen. Marya, whose eyes were the keenest, spotted what they were searching for beyond the abandoned office equipment. "Over there," she said pointing, "along that back wall."

Ravenwood and Stagg, who was still holding his candle, walked around the desks spreading the yellow glow even further; enough to recognize the cheap wooden coffins covering the floor before them.

"Holy crap!" Stagg gasped. "How many of them are there?" he asked while mentally trying to count.

"Eighteen," Ravenwood replied. "There are eighteen of them, Inspector. I suggest we start from the closest to us and work our way to the wall. That way, if any of them become …active…we'll be able to herd them in and cut off any means of escape they may have."

"What the hell do you mean by…active?"

It was Marya who explained further. "They are not sleeping, inspector. The undead can never really sleep. They rest now, unable to face the rays of the sun. So, even though they are weakened and vulnerable, in such a darkened place they might still have enough strength to react; to fight. None of your men must hesitate to do what must be done. Do you understand me?"

"I think so, lady." Stagg tilted his round derby back on his head. "But why don't you and Ravenwood here demonstrate it for us. That way there won't be any screw ups."

"Very well," Ravenwood agreed. By now officers Carter and Monroe had set the bag of instruments on one of the dirty desks. He went to it, rummaged through it and pulled out a mallet, several wooden stakes and a flask.

Returning to Marya, he handed her the silver flask while addressing Stagg. "Stay close to me with that candle." Then he looked over the inspector's shoulder at the anxious faces watching them. "You others grab tools and gather around, but not too closely and stay alert. This is going to be most unpleasant."

With that he walked over to the nearest coffin and knelt down on one knee beside it. Stagg stood behind him holding up the candle while Marya took a spot at the top of the long box and uncapped the flask in her hand.

She looked down at Ravenwood. "Ready when you are."

Without further preamble, the occult detective slammed the mallet upward along the side of the coffin catching the lip of the cover. It ripped up in one piece and fell to the floor opposite him. Inside was a female vampire dressed in moldy clothing and reeking of rotten meat, her colorless face smeared with pieces of vermin blood and gore.

Ravenwood leaned over and placed the sharpened tip of his wooden stake against her chest and began to raise the mallet over his head. Suddenly the vampire's dull red eyes opened and she snarled at the sight of him. She began to rise up only to have Marya lean over and spill Holy Water onto her face. It sizzled upon contact and the undead creature screamed in pain, her clawed hands going to her damaged face.

"Ready when you are."

It was all the diversion the Stepson of Mystery required as he slammed his hammer down with all his might and drove the stake into her heart. Blood bubbled up from the wound like a tiny geyser and the foul creature's body convulsed violently. Her hands tried to pull at the offending steak at which point, Marya reached into her cloak and brought forth her butcher's blade. With one powerful stroke she cleaved the vampire's head off its neck. The creature stopped moving...in true death.

Ravenwood reached in, took hold of the now lifeless monster's head by her hair and standing, held it aloft for all to see. "Make sure to remove their heads. It is the only sure way to guarantee they will never rise again." He then tossed it away to land with a plop yards away.

At the exact same time several of the coffins began to rattle as if something inside them was moving.

"They know we are here," Marya warned. "There is no time to waste."

"Yah heard the lady," Stagg growled. "Form up into pairs and get busy. All of you." The nearest coppers stood transfixed, some still staring at the headless body with the stake in its chest. "NOW!!!" Bellowed Stagg. "What dah hell do you think this is; a picnic?"

Jumping, the officers shook off their fears and began opening coffins.

"Come on," Stagg said to Ravenwood as he started towards another rattling coffin. "Let's get this freaking job over with."

—)|(—

Fifty feet away, hidden in an expediter's backroom alcove, Baron Henri Savigne heard the screams of his ghoulish pack and immediately knew they were under attack. He pushed up the cover to his more lavish coffin and sat up. Like all such mobile repositories, the satin cushions beneath him were covered with dirt from his French hometown. Quickly he climbed out and whipped his black cape about his shoulders. The noises from within the warehouse were growing louder. He could hear hammers pounding into cold flesh, the agonized screams of his children as they were set upon by unknown forces.

He moved through the darkness to a second, much larger coffin, set beside the room's single door. He hurriedly pried it open to reveal his loyal servant, Berleze.

"Get up," he whispered. "And be quiet. We are under attack."

Clumsily the big vampire pulled himself from his own crate-sized coffin just as there was a chorus off shouts coming from the main hall.

Both recognized them as human cries. They were followed by two loud gunshots.

Baron Savigne carefully opened the door and exited. To his right was the back door to the loading docks and back alleys. To his left was the warehouse itself and pressing himself against the wall he saw policemen moving about the coffins of his people like eerie death-dealing specters in the harsh flickering light of the moving candles.

But how had the authorities found them?

Then, as the light continued to move about he recognized the person with the hooded cloak. It was a woman…the woman! The countess herself! So that was how the police had found them out. The bitch had turned the tables on her hunters. She was as ruthless as she was clever, he mused. But now it became a matter of survival. There was no way he, even with Berleze's strength, could overcome that many hunters.

They had only one recourse; to find shelter. And they had to go now before they were discovered!

━━✦━━

Ravenwood held his Luger by his side ready for any other struggling vampires. The police had begun their work of destroying the odious beings and the first few went well enough. But when one pair opened the fifth coffin, the ravenous vampire inside lunged up at them before they could act. With frantic desperation he'd knocked down the officer with the mallet and stake and then sprung up out of the box and struck at the second man with his long sharpened nails. The cop's cheek was cut open and he fell back dropping his flask of Holy Water.

Like a maddened clown, the freed vampire had cackled and turned around eyeing its foes, hands out ready to wreak more destruction. Ravenwood had immediately dropped his own tools and rushed to confront the crazed killer. He had drawn his pistol from its shoulder rig and shot the thing in the head…twice. It collapsed in front of the two shaken coppers.

"See why you have to work fast," he reminded them holding his gun up. "Somebody help that officer and get those cuts on his face seen to. The rest of you keep at it!"

All of that had transpired in a less than a minute. Now the occult detective stood ready to assist any of the other teams should another bloodsucker prove too difficult to vanquish.

"Ravenwood!" Marya came up behind him and grabbed his elbow.
"What?"

"I thought a heard a door open and close back there, towards the rear of the building."

He looked over and could just make out the outlines of a door. "Are you sure?"

"Yes," she said clutching his arm. "Right after you fired your pistol. I think some of them may have escaped."

Seeing the worry on her face, Ravenwood had no choice but to believe her. He saw Stagg working with a pair of officers to open another coffin closer to the back wall and called out to him. "Stagg, some may have gotten out the back. We're going to check it out. You and your men keep at it."

The short inspector merely waved to him in acknowledgement as Ravenwood and Marya ran to the back of the building.

He was the first to reach the door and pulling it open was temporarily blinded by sunshine. He blinked several times and was stunned to see two figures hurrying down the middle of the alleyway. One was massive while the other was wrapped in a thick cape. Both of them were aflame as a gray smoke exuded from their bodies and their progress was clearly awkward and difficult.

"Dear God," Marya exclaimed as she came alongside of him and sighted the fleeing vampires. "Where are they running to? There is nowhere for them to hide."

But Marya was wrong. Ravenwood spotted the circular outline of a manhole cover in the middle of the street. That was obviously their goal; to get into the sewers away from the burning sun and then evade their pursuers.

Ravenwood fired at them but missed. Neither vampire looked back as both were totally focused on the round, heavy steel plate. Reaching it, the smaller of the two, turned and directed the big one to lift it up. In doing so his head was visible to Marya and she recognized him immediately.

"Baron Savigne! He was one of the men who approached us in Paris."

Despite the awful pain he was suffering, Berleze squeezed his fingers under the edge of the manhole lid and easily tore off the gaping hole beneath. Ravenwood fired again and hit the undead behemoth in the back. Grunting in pain, Berleze spun about and with a mighty heave hurled the manhole cover.

It spun through the air like a top straight for Ravenwood and Marya. Ravenwood tackled her to the pavement seconds before the deadly disc flew by. It crashed into a pile of old trashcans, mashing them as if they were made of cardboard.

On the ground, Ravenwood dared lift his head just in time to see the baron starting to drop into the sewer opening. He looked back at them, his face bubbling red and yelled up at the big vampire, "STOP THEM!"

"Yes, master." Berleze began to shamble towards Ravenwood and Marya. The unbearable heat was causing his entire body to combust with each stumbling step he took. But his dimwitted mind refused to accept his fate in carrying out his master's order.

Ravenwood, still prone on the rough tar of the alleyway pointed his Luger at the oncoming mass of fiery hell and fired three more rounds into it with seemingly no effect. Then, only a few yards from them, the monster staggered, raised its arms skyward and cried out in anguished doom before crashing down. Its entire body burst asunder becoming nothing but black ash and skeletal pieces within seconds. A gust of wind blew over the remains as the flames died out and all that was left of Berleze were his bones and smoldering tatters of his clothes.

Warily Ravenwood put away his gun and got to his feet at the same time helping Marya up. Together they approached the smoking shape.

"Give me your knife," Ravenwood said and Marya handed it over. With a fast stroke, the Stepson of Mystery detached the skull from the corpse and then kicked it down the alley. That done, the two of them approached the open manhole and peered down into its dark well.

"We have to go after him," Marya urged.

"I know. But we need a light. Or else we'll be sitting ducks down there."

"There's no time."

Ravenwood looked at the long, fat butcher's blade in his hand. "Then we'll have to improvise."

He raised the sharp cutting weapon and carefully put both his hands to either side of the clean, shiny blade. Then he closed his eyes and began to utter a Tibetan magic spell he had learned from the Nameless One. His voice was low as he softly repeated the foreign words over and over in a practiced cadence.

After a few seconds, the blade began to glow as if it held some inner electrical charge.

Marya's eyes widened in awe at what she was seeing. There was much more to her new ally than she had suspected.

Ravenwood opened his eyes to a glimmering blade as bright as any torch.

"Now we're ready." Marya nodded. "Stay close to me."

"Yes, but please, Ravenwood, let's hurry."

Ravenwood gave her the glowing knife and started to climb down the rusty ladder just inside the manhole opening. At chest level he opened his hand and she once again passed the deadly weapon to him and he descended completely out of sight.

Steadying her resolve with a deep breath, Marya removed her cumbersome cloak, tossed it aside and began down the ladder into the black depths below.

—⟫⟨—

Ravenwood stepped off the last rung of the ladder into fetid water that reached to his ankles—so much for his expensive Italian shoes. As Marya climbed down, he moved away from the ladder into the inky blackness around them, his feet making sloshing noises. The glowing butcher's cleaver illuminated the red brick walls that made up the long narrow tunnel that ran into two different directions from the manhole entrance. The air was both cool and foul, the water a sickly brown color.

"Be careful," he whispered as he used his free hand to assist Marya's last few downward steps. "There is water here and the floor beneath is slick."

The lovely brunette stepped down carefully holding on to his forearm. "Lovely. I wasn't expecting a tour of the city's nether regions." She wrinkled her nose. "And that smell is overripe as well."

"Methane," Ravenwood said. "It's a good thing we didn't bring in any candles. The gas is dangerously flammable."

Marya released his arm and put her index up over her lush lips to quiet him. She titled her head and listened. Ravenwood couldn't hear at thing. Then he too heard a splashing sound coming from the tunnel to their right.

"Yes," Marya softly agreed. "That way."

Taking the lead, his glowing knife before him, Ravenwood began moving down the waterway. As he walked, doing his best to minimize the noise of the water sucking at his feet, he recalled the history of the city's underground passages. Most of the current sewage tunnels had been constructed after the Civil War by returning veterans as the great urban metropolis' population continued to grow with the constant influx of immigrants from around the world. The then newly christened Board of Health saw the threat of open sewage ditches and thus collected tax revenues to construct a major underground system in which to properly dispose of human waste and rainwater runoff. Being situated on an island, it was all too convenient to have the waste flow dumped into the rivers and harbor.

After a few minutes, Ravenwood and Marya came to a central juncture that joined two tunnels and once again stopped to survey the area. Ravenwood could hear cascading water coming from the tunnel to their left. It seemed to curve slightly and then he smelled the pungent odor of brine. They had to be approaching the river.

He heard footsteps moving away in that very direction. He signaled Marya and began increasing his pace. If that was Baron Savigne ahead of them, Ravenwood guessed he was in for a surprise. Marya kept up with him, being careful not to slip as she too was weary of the dirty water.

When they came around the bend in the tunnel, the blade's knife illuminated Baron Henri Savigne standing at the edge of a twenty-foot precipice that dropped into a collecting pool alongside of a submerged iron grating beyond which extended a four foot pipe that jutted out over the river.

The baron spun around and without warning threw himself forward. He came off his feet and actually flew the ten-foot distance between them. Caught unprepared, Ravenwood was knocked backwards off his feet. In the process Marya was pushed into the wall banging her forehead. She collapsed in a swoon.

Savigne had landed atop the Stepson of Mystery and was now reaching for his throat with his hands while he opened his mouth to reveal his yellowish, extended fangs.

"Chase after me will you?" he spit out, drool falling from his open mouth. "I will make you suffer for such impudence."

Ravenwood, still dazed by the assault, raised his head out of the foul water just as the vampire lord's hands took hold of his neck and began to squeeze. He started to bring his hands up and realized the right still held Marya's butcher blade. Just as Savigne's head came down towards his face, Ravenwood swung out with the knife. The edge sliced across the vampire's open mouth from side to side, tearing the flesh in the process.

Savigne screamed and fell back on his legs as Ravenwood tried to sit up. Filled with rage, the vampire's left hand struck out and grabbing the blade tore it out of Ravenwood's hand and tossed it away.

"BASTARD!!!" he roared. "Now I will suck every drop of blood from your worthless body."

Baron Savigne once again pressed down on the struggling human, pushing down the struggling Ravenwood's head, shoving it back into the water with one hand while exposing his jugular. For Ravenwood only one thought remained; if this was to be his end he would not die easily. He continued to bat away at the ancient fiend as it began to lower its fangs into his neck.

But Savigne never finished his attack for at that very moment Marya rose up behind him holding her thick knife in both hands and drove it in to the vampire's back to the hilt. Again Savigne knew pain and reacted like the animal he was. He twisted about and backhanded Marya across the face propelling her back toward the lip of the tunnel's end.

He tried to reach behind to take hold of the offending blade but couldn't reach it no matter how hard he tried.

Jumping to his feet and ignoring Ravenwood completely, the French vampire pushed himself towards the semi-conscious woman.

"You bitch! All of this was your fault! You couldn't just accept your fate. You had to run and bring about this folly." As he drew closer, Savigne's mindless rage filled his thoughts with the indignities he had been made to suffer because of Marya Dracula. "As if you could ever hope to win out. Foolish, stupid bitch!"

Standing over her, Baron Savigne reached down, grabbed a handful of Marya's hair and pulled her head up roughly. She moaned in pain.

"Time to die."

"NOOOOO!" Ravenwood came out of the darkness behind Savigne and tackled him causing him to let go of Marya and together they fell over the edge.

Into the catch pool they plunged all the way to its cement bottom only three feet deep.

Ravenwood lost his breath under the water but kept his hold on the vampire. Now Savigne was thrashing and somehow manage to find his feet so that he erupted out of the salty water in pure panic.

Salt! Ravenwood broke the surface and gasped for air. Of course, the Hudson was an estuary and it flowed both ways; fresh water from the north, salt water from the south. And it was this element that was consuming Baron Savigne. Just as the table salt had destroyed the vampire back in the diner the previous evening, so the Atlantic brine was having the same affect on the baron. Crazily he tried to pull at the iron grading facing the exit pipe as to climb out of the deadly water but Ravenwood wouldn't let him.

With what strength he had left, he reached up and pulled the vampire back into the pool and then fell over him. It was like riding a slippery seal as Savigne flopped around in the burning pool, the flesh coming off his body in huge chunks. He managed to push Ravenwood off once but his face was nearly gone. Ravenwood felt him weakening and again pulled him down. There was one final convulsion and then the monster stopped moving. Holding him down, Ravenwood came out of the water and took a gulp of air. There was no more movement under his hands.

Releasing his hold, he watched as what remained of Baron Savigne floated to the surface. Most of the flesh had been burned away and only the skeletal frame was visible under the baron's clothing. Though almost totally exhausted, the Stepson of Mystery reached over and pulled the butcher's knife free and then turning the floating corpse around, held the skull while he cut it off at the neck. Once done, he moved to the iron bars and shoved it through one of the square gaps. It was washed away and out the pipe's other end.

"Are you alright?"

Ravenwood turned from the grating and looked up at Marya, kneeling near the tunnel's edge. Her face was bloodied and there were a few bruises he could make out. Luckily his spell on the knife was still active and lit the space.

"I think so."

"Is there a way out of the pool?"

Ravenwood sloshed across the pool to the wall and holding the blade was thankful to see small iron rungs welded into it. "Yes. Hold on."

Slowly, his feet slippery on the rungs, he climbed up to the tunnel floor and there Marya helped him over the lip where they both fell back and sat in silence, wet and cold...and mercifully alive.

Finally she turned to him, wiping a smear of blood off her cheek with her soaked sleeve of her dress and smiled. "Thank you."

Ravenwood looked at her face in the eerie light of the blade, here in this dungeon-like place and thought it was the most beautiful thing he had ever seen.

He touched her bruised cheek and leaned forward to kiss her.

Marya started to pull away only to look into his eyes. One was blue and one was green. Both held only warmth and love.

He leaned in again and their lips touched.

—*≺·≻*—

TWO MONTHS LATER –

The wind at the top of the world was always crying as it slipped through the ragged jutting teeth of the Himalayas. It was a mournful howl mostly unheard above five thousand feet where a desolate landscape of white threatened any that dared venture up into its frozen solitude.

Three such fools clung to the side of a mountain pass working their way along a rock ledge as the wind tugged at their burdensome clothing. Cleated boots came down purposefully wary of icy patches that could send the climber spiraling off into space and to a sure death far, far below amidst the gaping chasms.

At the lead, Ravenwood moved with his torso leaning forward, his face all but hidden by a heavy woolen scarf and furred hood. He, like Marya and Jazzy, wore goggles to protect his eyes from the bitter cold. They were tied together by a coarse horsehair rope given to them by the Sherpa guides who had accompanied them to the midpoint in their journey.

Courage, my son, you are almost there. The voice of the Nameless One was still present inside his mind and Ravenwood could not help but marvel at his mentor's mental prowess.

It had been the Nameless One's idea all along after Ravenwood, Marya and Stagg's police detachment had cleaned up the vampire nest at the dockside warehouse. All of them assumed that when Baron Savigne failed to report to the Imperial Vampire Court others would be dispatched to find Marya and her daughter. The undead would never give up. Thus it was paramount that they find a sanctuary where they would be safe from their foes; a place no evil could ever discover or overcome.

That place was the Hidden City where the Nameless One had brought Ravenwood when he was a child and there, with other monks, taught him all manners of oriental philosophies and magics. Thus, when he had put forth the idea, the Stepson of Mystery knew it was the only logical solution.

So had begun their long journey crossing the Pacific by luxury liner and then crossing the vast breadth of China by rail until reaching Nepal and the city of Kathmandu three days ago. Here Ravenwood had hired two Sherpa guides and the final leg of their trek began on a frigid, October day.

To their credit, both Marya and Jazzy had endured the arduous climb with silent strength, though he could see in their faces that they were both physically drained. They plodded along behind him like sleepwalkers following his lead unwaveringly. When the path they were on entered into a hidden cave in the mountain, all of them were relieved to be out of the brutal wind.

"How are you both doing?" Ravenwood leaned back against the cave's interior wall and pulled the stiff scarf from his face.

Marya did the same before replying. "Please, tell me we don't have much further to go." He could see the hint of doubt in her green eyes and it bothered him that they would soon be parting company. The intimacy they had shared these past week had been precious to both of them.

"The Nameless One is still in contact with me." He pointed a gloved hand to his head. "He says we are almost there and he's right. Though it's been ten years since I was here."

"Tell me they have hot food there?' Jazzy begged. She was aware of the change in the relationship between her mother and Ravenwood and mischievously teased Marya whenever he wasn't present.

My son, do not stop. You must keep moving.

"That and much, much more," he said and then pushed away from the wall. "Let's go."

He led them through the cave, which opened to another chasm across which was a small wooden bridge. On the other side was another cave.

Without stopping, Ravenwood crossed the snow-covered span and entered the second cave. He continued to move through the spacious opening until finally the air about them began to feel warm. Ten minutes later it was hot as they reached a huge opening and found themselves looking down at one of the most unique vistas in the entire world.

There stretched out below them was a long valley split by a winding river. There were green hills and forest to either side and they could make out the thatched roofs of small villages.

"Oh, my God," Marya removed her scarf and hood. Then she pulled off her goggles. The others did the same. "Is this place real or are we hallucinating?"

"Oh, it's very real, I assure." Ravenwood smiled happily. Then he pointed to the left where a wide dirt road from the valley went up to a fantastic complex of snow-white buildings. "That's the monastery, where you'll be staying. It was my home once."

Marya and Jazzy held hands and looked down on the white buildings, each surrounded by lush, colorful gardens.

"It's like the Garden of Eden," Jazzy suggested. "Look, someone is coming!"

A bald headed monk in a brown robe and wearing sandals was riding up a winding path to them on the back of a burro. When he reached them, he slid off his mount and greeted them.

"We've been expecting you, Ravenwood. It is good to see you again." He turned and smiled at Marya and Jazzy. "I am Brother Thaddeus. Welcome to Shangri-La."

THE END

YOU *CAN* GO HOME AGAIN

Fifteen years ago I wrote a 108 page graphic novel script called "The Daughter of Dracula." In it, Marya Dracula, the only surviving heir of the infamous vampire, Count Dracula, met a young German lad named Manfred von Richthofen just prior to the start of World War One. She at that time was a 500 year old vampire and became infatuated with the young man; enough to keep tabs on him when the war broke out. Of course von Richthofen, a real historical figure, was to go on to become the most deadly German aviation ace of them all nicknamed the Red Baron.

Marya travels to Berlin at the height of his fame and seduces him thus beginning a torrid love affair that last until von Richthofen is actually shot down and killed. Marya is enraged by his death and declares war against the allied pilots...until she discovers she is actually pregnant with Manfred's child; that pregnancy ends her curse and she is human once again; no longer a vampire. The book closes with Marya leaving Transylvania behind, very much pregnant and looking forward to starting her new, fully human life again with her child.

Nine years ago artist Rob Davis read that script and decided he wanted to bring it to visual life. It would take him two years to complete the project. Thus seven years ago we self-published "The Daughter of Dracula" via Rob's own imprint, Redbud Studio and it has gone on to much critical acclaim. We continue to sell it at Amazon and personally at our convention appearancse and its audience continues to grow. People are surprised by the book's positive ending and the honest romance at the core of the tale. Which pleases Rob and me greatly.

Anyway, up until a few months ago I thought Marya's story was finished. Although as her creator, there was always that part of me that wondered what had happened to her after the end of the graphic novel. Did she have the baby? Was it a boy or a girl? Where did they go to live out their lives? Those questions have buzzed around in my noggin for the past seven years. Then out of the blue, writer Josh Reynolds suggested we do an anthology starring occult detectives. Just like that we had Joel Jenkins and Jim Beard on board. Each of these three talented writers had their own heroes, which they had invented; whereas we needed one more tale to fill the book. Which was when I got the idea of writing a Ravenwood – Stepson of Mystery adventure. Airship 27 had already done two anthologies with the hero and I was particularly eager to try my own hand at writing him.

But what would I write? And then, as so often happens, the muse began talking to me. What if Marya Dracula came to New York City with her child and crossed paths with Ravenwood? But why? Because they were being chased by vampires….and then just like a row of dominoes falling one atop the other, the plot to "Jazzy," exploded full blown in my imagination and there she was…Marya and Manfred's child, now a beautiful, spunky teenage girl. From that point on I couldn't write this story fast enough. I pray you enjoyed it and if you haven't read "Daughter of Dracula," will go out and pick up a copy. Whereas if you are a dedicated fan of that graphic novel, I hope you liked seeing Marya again and meeting Jazemara Dracula.

For me, it was very much like coming home again.

RON FORTIER - A veteran comic book creator, he's best known for writing the Green Hornet and Terminator:Burning Earth, with Alex Ross, for Now Comics back in the 90s. Today, he keeps busy writing and editing new pulp anthologies and novels via his Airship 27 Productions (http://robmdavis.com/Airship27Hangar/airship27hangar.html). He won the Pulp Factory Award for Best Pulp Short Story of 2011 for "Vengeance Is Mine" which appeared in *The Avenge – Justice Inc.* from Moonstone Books and again in 2012 for "The Ghoul," which appeared in *Monster Aces.*

He continues to write his own graphic novels and series, such as Mr. Jigsaw Man of a Thousands Parts via Redbud Studio. (http://www.robmdavis.com/RedbudStudio/index.html)

You can keep updated with his latest projects by visiting his personal website at: (www.airship27.com)

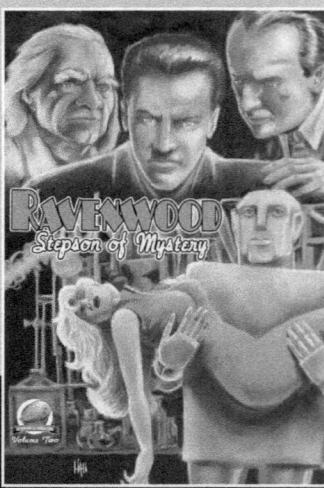

Situated in the rural back country of Edwardian England is an old, mysterious house whose unique owner earns his living as a Spirit-Breaker, a hunter of ghosts. A former military veteran, Sgt. Roman Janus has devoted his life to aid those haunted, both emotionally and physically by obsessive wraiths whose spirits are still anchored to our world.

Airship 27 Productions is thrilled to present *Sgt. Janus – Spirit Breaker* by Jim Beard. Part detective, part occultist, Janus is himself a man of mystery whose own past is shrouded and the motivations behind his calling kept hidden. Within this volume you will find eight tales as narrated by his clients, each with his or her own perspective on this uncanny hero and his amazing career. Filled with suspense, terror and agonizing pathos, each a solid mesmerizing journey into the unknown world beyond.